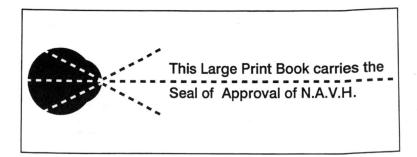

This Large Print Book carries the
Seal of Approval of N.A.V.H.

FINAL CURTAIN

MIGNON F. BALLARD

Thorndike Press • Thorndike, Maine

Library of Congress Cataloging in Publication Data:

Ballard, Mignon Franklin.
   Final curtain / Mignon F. Ballard.
     p. cm.
   ISBN 1-56054-579-8 (alk. paper : lg. print)
   1. Large type books. I. Title.
[PS3552.A466F56   1993]   92-34318
813'.54—dc20   CIP

Thorndike Large Print® Romance Series edition published in 1993 by arrangement with Carroll & Graf Publishers, Inc.

Cover photo by Tom Knobloch.

The tree indicium is a trademark of Thorndike Press.

This book is printed on acid-free, high opacity paper. ∞

For Mimi

Chapter One

I heard the piano across the lawn, a jangling ragtime tune with a carousel sound. The lighted windows of Plumb-Nelly Tavern looked welcoming in the dusk, and low, comfortable laughter drifted to meet me from the wide front porch. Someone was watching. I knew it, felt it.

The group of people gathered there feigned disinterest in my approach, yet I knew they hadn't missed a thing. Mama Kate, my grandmother, had warned me to be careful here. But careful of what? Was it because of this house — this place where my aunt was killed? What if Mama Kate was right? Something awful had happened here — could happen again. For some reason I felt the need to hurry.

The big rocking chairs had been painted gray, but I knew they were the same ones I had sat in as a child when my feet barely touched the floor. Were the people the same too? The man who sat on the porch railing casually stripping dead fronds from a potted fern seemed slightly familiar. He looked to be in his mid-seventies and wore a rumpled tan sweater, and khaki pants with grass-stained knees. At least the atmosphere wasn't going to be formal.

I hurried inside to wash my hands, nodding to the three people who had watched my progress. Did they know why I was here?

I wondered if the tavern's owner would remember me as the little red-haired pest from sixteen years ago. I hadn't yet seen Bailey Davenport, but his older sister, Delaney, who had registered me earlier, stood in the entrance hall chatting with guests and looking every bit as beautiful as she had at fifteen. Her red-fringed scarf and bright print skirt gave her a Gypsy-like appearance, but her laughter sounded almost sad; it reminded me of an anguished heroine's from an old movie. She didn't recognize me, of course. I was only ten when I stayed here last, and the name Virginia Cameron obviously meant nothing to her.

I stopped for a minute at the top of the stairs, admiring the spacious hall below with its rich paneling and polished brass fixtures. And for a few seconds I found myself being swept up in an invisible tide surging between the past and the present. I knew then this strange insistent tugging would carry me along whether I wanted to go or not.

When I came downstairs a group had gathered around the piano in the room they called the front parlor, where a tall young man pounded out "Wait Till the Sun Shines, Nellie" with a rinky-tink beat. I smiled. My grandmother would have loved it. The pianist smiled back at me and switched to a jazzed-up version of "For Me and My Gal." His eyes never left my face. I had seen him earlier trimming the chrysanthemums in the flower bed out front.

One of the would-be singers turned and beckoned me to join them, making room for me at his side. Bailey Davenport. The owner of Plumb-Nelly had dark hair like his sister's and carried a paperback book — one of Carl Sagan's, I think — in the pocket of his worn corduroy blazer. And as Mama Kate says, he couldn't find a tune in a bank vault if you gave him the combination.

I waited until we filed into the dining room to give him the first clue. "I don't suppose we're having blackberry cobbler?" I said. "Or gingerbread with hard sauce?"

He pulled out a chair for me at the long table and sat beside me with a curious look on his face. Except for a tinge of gray at his hairline, Bailey's hair was almost blue-black, and he still had a faint scar over his left brow from the time he had fallen out of his tree house. "Didn't get many blackberries last summer," he said. "Too dry. And we haven't had hard sauce since Maggie left."

"And where is Maggie?" This certainly wasn't good news.

"Living in Raleigh with her daughter. She's pushing ninety, you know." He frowned. "You knew Maggie?"

"I'll say! She always let me lick the bowls." I sipped from my water goblet. "So, what would I have to do to get extra desserts around here?"

Awareness eased over his handsome face like a smile. "You're not! You are, aren't you? That piggy little girl who stayed here one summer. You're Ginger." His hand reached for my hair, then stopped. "You always seemed to have cockleburs in your hair and dirt on your face." Bailey Davenport laughed. "You look much better without them."

"I guess I was pretty much of a pest following you around like I did. Sorry about that."

He passed around a platter of country ham and smiled as I took a fair-sized slice. "You can follow me around anytime," he said.

The man with the grass-stained pants who sat on my right extended a hand after he heaped his plate. He was a large man, but not at all fat, and I wondered how he stayed trim eating such huge portions. "I'm Kirby Whitworth, Bailey's uncle, and I grew those sweet potatoes you just passed up. I think you should at least give them a fair trial."

"Uncle Kirby grows most of the vegetables we serve now that he's given up being mayor," Bailey explained. "And what we can't get from his garden we buy from Otto here. He owns The Store."

"The store?"

I couldn't quite picture the frail, middle-aged man across from me wearing a big white apron and measuring out dried beans. "That's what everybody has always called it, so the name just stuck," he told me. "Of course, it's not the only one in town, but we do sell pretty much everything."

Kirby Whitworth leaned toward me and whispered loud enough for all to hear, "If you eat it, drink it, wear it, or float it in your cow pond, Otto Millsap has it."

The man across from me expertly cut another bite of ham, skewered it with one green bean and a slice of beet, then chewed slowly, never taking his eyes from his plate. I thought it was probably a good thing Uncle Kirby wasn't running for mayor anymore, because he wasn't going to get Otto's vote.

Kirby Whitworth smiled and shrugged. "Ah, well, rude am I in my speech, and little blessed with the soft phrase of peace . . . sorry."

I glanced at Bailey for an explanation, but he only laughed and shook his head.

After a dessert of raspberry sherbet and sugar cookies with just a faint taste of coriander, everybody gradually left the table. Delaney nodded with kind of a curious little smile as she passed us on the way to the kitchen, but Bailey delayed her. "You'll never guess who this is," he said to her, pulling me to my feet. "Just think back a few years."

"Bailey, you know I'm not good at guessing games." Delaney took a tiny step in place in her impatience to leave.

"The summer of the pink bikini," he said. And to my surprise, his sister laughed.

"Dad wouldn't let me wear it to the pool, so I sunbathed in it," she explained.

I remembered. Every morning for an hour or two Delaney had sunned in a deck chair behind the house and painted her nails with a flaming pink polish hot enough to set the house on fire. "Strawberry Sundae," I said.

"What?" Gold bracelets clanked as she ran a hand over her hair, a habit I remembered from years before. She did it when she was nervous about something. Or worried.

"That was the color. You painted your nails with it. And you wore the lipstick too. It

12

smelled like strawberries."

"Good Lord! I do remember you," Delaney said. "You're the one who ate all those desserts. Seven chocolate cupcakes at one sitting! Maggie said she'd never seen anything like it."

Why did everybody make such a big deal over what a pig I was? "I think she exaggerated," I said. "But I remember your doing my hair in a French braid. I wore it like that for three days — wouldn't undo it."

"Well, I see you've learned how to handle it on your own." Delaney glanced at the back of my hair and looked almost approving. On busy days I gathered it up in one long braid just to get it out of my way, and this had been one of those times.

Delaney glanced toward the kitchen. "I have to go over tomorrow's menus with Ethelene before she gets away. Are you staying long? Maybe we'll have a chance to talk longer before you go."

About what? I wondered, watching her walk away. The gap in our ages had narrowed now that we were both adults, but other than the few early memories we shared, we really didn't have a lot in common. I didn't think I could ever feel close to Delaney Davenport. I wondered if anyone did.

A large calico cat stretched, then curled into

a spotted ball by the fireplace in the front parlor. It was a long, gracious room done in shades of deep turquoise and rose with accents of pale yellow; a concert piano dominated the corner near the dining room, and the same man who had played earlier shuffled through a stack of sheet music in the bench. "I'm all for the old favorites," he said, brandishing a yellowing booklet, "but don't you people have at least one piece of music published since 1938?"

Bailey glanced at the tattered collection and shrugged. "Sorry. Delaney never made it through John Thompson's Second Book and I was too hopeless to even begin, but if you'll tell me what you need, I'll pick some up in Morganton.

"This is Rob Quillian, our resident musician and handyman," he said to me. "He's modest, of course, but he can do just about anything that needs doing."

Suddenly the gangling pianist didn't seem to know what to do with his hands. And was he actually shuffling his feet? Good Lord, how big were his feet? They seemed oddly out of proportion to the rest of him.

"Should I break into song and dance?" It was hard to tell from the glint in his gray eyes if Rob Quillian was annoyed or merely teasing. "Or would you prefer a recitation? Maybe

14

I could practice my juggling . . ."

"What did I tell you?" Bailey shook his head. "Rob, this is Ginger, a woman from my sordid past."

"Who happens to have some current sheet music," I said. "It might not be what you like, but you're welcome to it."

"At this point I'm not choosy. Where is it?" Rob dumped the pile of music back into the stool and banged the lid.

"In the trunk of my car. Just give me a minute to get my keys."

"Wouldn't you like me to go with you?" Rob asked. "It's pretty dark out there."

I started to brush aside his offer. This was Fiddler's Glen, North Carolina, the place where I had spent what was probably my happiest summer, and aside from my family, no one even knew I was here. Did they? I looked at the long windows that opened onto the porch, and except for the reflection of firelight, all I could see was darkness. Was he out there somewhere? Waiting? "Sure," I said. "If you don't mind."

Bailey would have followed us, I think, if a frightening-looking hawk-nosed woman presiding over a card table near the windows hadn't snared his arm. "You haven't introduced me," she said, drumming long, red nails on the table.

I thought Bailey was going to laugh, but he didn't. "How can I live with such an oversight?" he said with a perfectly straight face. "Mrs. Tyler Stafford-Smith, I'd like you to meet Miss Virginia Cameron, an old friend of mine. She's going to be staying with us this week."

"Eugenia," the woman said. "Call me Eugenia. Sit down." She indicated the empty chair. The other two were occupied by Bailey's uncle Kirby and Otto Millsap, both of whom seemed to be having a fine time at my expense.

Part of me was insulted at the authority the woman assumed, but the coward in me had already started to sit at command, when somebody tugged at my arm. I think it was Rob.

He smiled and kissed her hand — so heavy with rings it must have weighed ten pounds. "The lady has another errand right now, Eugenia. You'll just have to get in line."

She looked right past him. "You play bridge?" Her piercing black eyes impaled me. Dark brows arched under sleek jet hair coiled in a crown at the top of her head. She wore a long black skirt and matching cape. It was like looking into a coal cellar. The only relief was her heavily rouged cheeks, starched white blouse, and an oval locket on a heavy gold chain. She scared me to death.

16

"Well, do you?" she demanded, shuffling the cards without taking her eyes from me.

"I played a little with my grandparents, but only if they threatened me," I told her. "I'm not very good. I'm not good at all."

"You'll learn." She took a sip of steaming pink liquid from a fragile cup, then waved me aside. "Oh, go on! Bailey can take your place tonight . . . and this time don't lead from a king," she told him. "Everybody always knows."

I didn't even feel guilty about leaving him there, but hurried after Rob into the hallway, where I hugged the newel post for support. "Does she fly away on Halloween?" I asked.

Rob laughed. "No such luck. With Eugenia it's Halloween all year round."

"She lives here?"

He nodded. "You'll get used to her; I did. We've declared a truce. Eugenia doesn't expect me to play bridge and I don't expect her to perform at the piano."

He waited while I went upstairs for my keys and we walked outside together. "Do you play the piano?" he asked as I shifted the heavy box of music into his arms.

"Some. I prefer the flute."

I could see the big smile on his face even in the dark. "Great! Maybe we could go through some of this together. I'm desperate

17

for some variation. What do you say?"

I laughed. "How do you know I can play?"

"All right, then, sing," he said. "I know you can sing because I heard you earlier. You have a very nice voice."

I made the usual polite noises without committing myself. I'm not crazy about impromptu parlor performances.

Rob was silent until we reached the front steps. Inside I could see Bailey patiently following his uncle's lead. He didn't seem to be having much fun. "Unless, of course, you'd rather play bridge," Rob reminded me.

"Which do you prefer?" I asked. "Rodgers and Hammerstein or Lionel Richie?"

Inside, Rob eagerly spread the sheet music on the piano, and chose first one, then another before finally deciding on Simon and Garfunkel's "The Sound of Silence." I nudged the cat aside and warmed myself at the fire while he played through the music. The bridge foursome in the corner ignored us and I was glad. But in spite of the awesome presence of Mrs. T.S.S., I sensed a serenity in the old parlor. I felt welcome here.

And then I saw the portrait. It was an oil painting of a girl in a porch swing and it hung in the shadows on the other side of the fireplace. The young woman in the picture seemed familiar. Where had I seen her before? And then I remembered. It had been in that same swing on the upstairs porch. She had stayed here the summer I was ten, although I had never met her. Every day in the late afternoon as I walked across the lawn from the swimming pool I would see her there swinging, and she always smiled at me. I was disappointed that we didn't meet because she had red hair like mine.

"I remember that girl," I said to Bailey as he paused to jot down the score. "She was here that same summer we were. Who is she? A relative?"

He smiled at me. Obviously I was forgiven for abandoning him to Eugenia. "What girl?"

"The one in the portrait over here. I used to see her on the upstairs porch."

Everything was quiet except for the song Rob was playing, which seemed even sweeter than usual. *In restless dreams I walked alone* . . . And then Bailey quickly picked up his cards and laughed. It was a soft kind of laugh, the kind you give to ease somebody over a mistake. And I knew the mistake was mine.

"You must have had a good imagination," Bailey said at last. "The girl in that portrait's been dead over fifty years."

Eugenia fanned out her cards and announced a no trump, then slowly met my gaze. "Unless she's seen the ghost."

19

Chapter Two

"What ghost?" I said.

"The one in the picture, I guess. Some claim to have heard it. To tell the truth, she looks vaguely familiar to me. Sometimes I think I might've seen her myself." Mrs. T.S.S. examined the dummy hand with a gloomy face.

"In a house as old as this one I'd be surprised if there wasn't a ghost," Rob said. "Good Lord, the place is probably packed with them!" He reared back on the piano bench, and with a soulful expression rendered a few trilling measures of the "Funeral March."

"Ignore them, Ginger," Bailey said, snatching a card trick from Eugenia's greedy clutches. "If Plumb-Nelly were haunted, believe me, I'd know it."

Eugenia sniffed. "I'm only repeating what I heard."

"And what was that?" Kirby Whitworth's eyebrows went up, and I saw him smile at his nephew.

"Mercer Belle Abernathy said she *saw* that swing squeaking back and forth up there one night when there wasn't a breath of wind, and not a soul in sight!" Eugenia snapped down her card with a vengeance. "And there were footsteps too — a woman's footsteps, she said."

"Mercer Belle Abernathy! My Lord, the woman still writes fan letters to Elvis Presley." Bailey's uncle Kirby clutched his cards to his chest. "Next thing you know, she'll have her rattling chains and moaning."

"Well, she's not the only one who heard it," Mrs. T.S.S. told him, drawing herself into an upright fortress. "Those two ladies who were here last summer — remember? The sisters from Wisconsin? Anyway, they swear there was somebody swinging out there." She drained her cup and made a smacking sound.

Rob immediately hunched over the keyboard and pounded out "I Ain't Got Nobody." I giggled.

I sat on the rug and invited the cat onto my lap. She felt soft and solid and warm. "Hasn't anybody ever seen her?" I asked.

Otto laid his cards aside. "Not that I know of, but my mother knew her."

Bailey frowned. "Knew who?"

"That girl in the painting. She worked here one summer; it was back in the thirties before my parents were married, and Mother had a job helping out in the kitchen. It was Depression time, you know. I forget the girl's name, but she was here with a bunch of actors doing summer stock. All as wild as Indians, Mother said, and that red-haired girl was the wildest of the lot — had a smart mouth too, from all I've heard."

"Your mother still calls a leg a 'limb' and a chicken thigh a 'second joint,' " Eugenia said. "Grace Millsap wouldn't know *wild* if it ran down the road with its pants on fire."

Otto's gray-tinged mustache fairly bristled. "Now, look here, Eugenia," he began. "I know you and Mother don't see eye to eye, but, you'll have to admit, she always tries to do right. Just as I do."

"And I suppose that includes selling those ghastly floating candles," Eugenia said. She turned to look at me over her shoulder. "Shaped like angels, and big as a dinner plate. You were supposed to float them in your lily pond or whatever." Her laugh wasn't exactly a cackle, but it was close.

"I had several on our lake out front last Christmas," Otto said, "and the effect was almost breathtaking."

"Looked like the whole damn pond was on fire," Mrs. T.S.S. muttered. "And then they sank. Just like lead. I'll bet you have thirty pounds of wax in the bottom of that water hole, Otto. It's a good thing poor Charlotte couldn't see it."

Otto Millsap smiled, but his hands gripped the corners of the table. "I like to think that my dear wife is very much aware of my earthly activities; in fact, I'm sure she's smiling down on us right now." And he took off his glasses to punctuate his remarks. Or maybe he just didn't want to look at Eugenia.

I couldn't really blame him. The shiny black topknot quivered as the woman leaned over the table. "Well, I certainly hope there are better things to do up there than look at you!" she said. "And if there isn't, you can be sure as hell that Charlotte isn't smiling."

Otto quickly jammed his glasses back in place as if he thought Eugenia might suddenly jump up and punch him; I wouldn't be surprised if she had. "I see no need —"

"I hate to bring an end to this fascinating debate," Bailey said, glancing at the clock on the mantel, "but it is getting kind of late, and I have an early day tomorrow."

Rob looked up from the piano. "Stay awhile," he said to me as the bridge players scattered. "Sing something."

"Won't we keep people awake?"

"Not a chance. These old walls are thick, built to withstand arrows — bullets too, I guess. I doubt if they can hear us upstairs.

23

Now, you first. What do you want to try?"
He flipped through a thick sheaf of music.

Mrs. T.S.S. paused in the doorway to say good night. "I hope you won't take seriously what I said about that girl in the picture," she said with what might pass for a smile. "One of these days I'll remember where I saw her." I heard her going upstairs, tapping each step with her gold-headed cane. I don't know why she carried one; she didn't seem to rely on it. Otto Millsap and Bailey's uncle Kirby left in separate cars, the former rather huffily, I thought.

Otto's wife, Charlotte, who had died in an automobile accident a few years before, was a niece of Eugenia's, Rob explained, and Mrs. T.S.S. hadn't forgiven him for letting it happen.

"Was it really his fault?" I asked.

Rob shook his head. "No, but Charlotte was running an errand for Otto's mother. Grace Millsap's the most demanding woman in the world — and the biggest hypochondriac. Charlotte had gone to pick up a prescription for her at the drugstore when the accident happened. It was icy, and her car skidded into a tree down at that awful curve. Everybody calls it Oh My God Boulevard." He played a couple of scores of "Endless Love" and trailed his fingers down the keys.

"At least they tell me that's how it happened. I've only been here myself since March."

He looked up and smiled at my unspoken question. "The city and I came to an agreement of peaceful coexistence," he told me. "I decided life would be a lot more peaceful if I existed somewhere else — so here I am."

"For how long?"

He shrugged. "Who knows? Maybe a year. Maybe longer. Bailey and I have an arrangement. I take care of the landscaping and entertain the guests, and he gives me room and board. What more can you ask than that?"

I thought it sounded pretty good, and said so.

"Then stay. They could use some help in the dining room, and we'll give them their money's worth at the piano."

I laughed. "But I already have a job."

"Where? Doing what?" His hand crashed down on a chord. "No, wait! Let me guess. You're a model? No, a buyer. You work for one of those big department stores; one where you can't get anybody to wait on you."

I shook my head. "Wrong."

"A flight attendant? Travel agent!"

"Nope."

"You're a teacher . . . junior high English, and all the boys are in love with you."

"I hate to disillusion you. I'm in advertising: the selling side, for *The Shell City Dispatch*."

"Never heard of it."

"It's in Florida," I said. "My stepfather owns it."

He frowned. "How did you wind up all the way up here?"

"We stayed here once when I was ten," I said. "A whole summer. I just wanted to come back."

"By yourself? Why?"

"Why not?" I flipped through the music. "Let's do something from *My Fair Lady*. How about 'Wouldn't It Be Loverly?'"

He took the music from me and braced it in front of him, then ran through the first few bars in the treble clef. "When you think it's time to tell somebody what you're running from, you'll find I'm a pretty good listener."

Good Lord, was I that obvious? I managed a feeble excuse for a laugh and made a face. "What?"

"Out in the parking lot tonight. You were as nervous as a long-tailed cat in a room full of rocking chairs." He stared at me so long, I found myself wanting to look away. "Just remember what I said. Okay?"

"Okay," I said. "Now, shut up and play."

A blast of cool air hit me as we finished the song, and Bailey stepped in from the porch and raced the cat for the chair by the dying fire. It was a tie. "Beautiful," he said, looking at me. "I didn't know you could sing." The calico curled on Bailey's stomach, and he slowly stroked the fur on her neck and closed his eyes. "Don't let me stop you," he said, yawning.

"I thought you had an early day tomorrow," Rob said.

"I always have an early day. I just get tired of hearing those two bicker . . . Quit it, Agnes!" Bailey detached the cat's claws from his sweater and set her on the floor.

"Agnes?" I smiled.

"Delaney named her. Said she looks just like a woman who used to come here. Agnes somebody or other — had one of those spotted imitation fur coats and kind of a pinkish nose." He reached for a peppermint in the jar beside him and took a long time removing the wrapper. "You were joking about seeing the girl in that painting, weren't you?"

"Could've been somebody who looked like that, but she really does seem familiar. Who is she?" I had to make myself appear only mildly interested. I knew now who the girl was in the portrait. She was my great-aunt.

The one who disappeared. I had grown up hearing about this woman — her daring, her love of fun. She was almost like a fairy tale, and I was here to find out why she died. Somehow, I knew I had to do it soon.

"Well, Otto was right about her working here. She was an actress who lived here for a while. But that was a long time ago, back when we had a theater, way before I was born. The old building's still here, used to be a barn."

Rob stood and walked to the window. "What happened to her?" he asked.

"Aunt Lucy said she died in an accident — wandered off the side of a cliff. They couldn't locate her family, so she's buried out back in the old family plot." He glanced at the painting, and then at me. "You have hair just like her, you know."

What could I say to that? I was glad when Bailey continued. "Aunt Lucy will be glad we've finally found her sister. A new road's coming through next spring, and we're having to move the grave, so I advertised in a magazine. Dahlia Brown is finally going home." He stood to bank the fire with ashes. "She and my aunt were good friends. It's always bothered her that she wasn't able to get in touch with her relatives."

I arranged all the music in a neat stack. "Where is your aunt?"

"Went with a group on a tour of Europe. Uncle Kirby wouldn't go. He's such an old stay-at-home! She ought to be back in a few weeks though."

"I didn't know your uncle was married," I said. "Somehow I assumed he always eats here."

Bailey laughed. "He does most of the time. And if you ever ate my aunt Lucy's cooking, you'd know why."

"Frankly, I think she does it on purpose. Aunt Lucy's no fool." Delaney stood in the doorway with a bright shawl wrapped about her, her cheeks ruddy from the cold. I hadn't heard her come in, but the taillights of the car that had brought her hesitated at the end of the drive, then disappeared.

Delaney tossed her wrap on the back of a chair and poured a glass of wine from the decanter on the secretary. "If I'd had known you were having a party, I'd have come home earlier," she said, noticing the stack of music on the piano. "What've I missed?"

"Ginger thinks Plumb-Nelly's haunted," Bailey told her. "She's seen a red-haired ghost."

His sister smiled and took a sip of wine. "Oh, really? When?"

I glared at Bailey, who smiled back innocently. "That wasn't what I said at all. I said I saw the girl in the painting — or someone who looked like her, and it was years ago, the summer we stayed here."

"Well, it couldn't have been Dahlia Brown," Delaney said, going over to look at the painting. "Uncle Chamblee painted this in the summer of 1936, only a few weeks before she was killed. It must have been somebody else." She frowned. "Funny, though; I don't remember anybody like that here that summer. Where did you see her?"

"She was in a swing," I said. "Green wicker — just like the one in the picture — on the upstairs porch, near the far end, where the wisteria grew."

"What wisteria? You must have us mixed up with another place," Delaney said. "There's never been wisteria on that porch, at least not that I can remember. And the swing's on the other side, but it's the plain wooden kind. Gray. We've never had a wicker swing — green or otherwise."

"Then why did your uncle paint one?" Rob stood behind me to get a closer look at the picture. "And look at this shading behind her. Could be wisteria."

I laughed. "Hey, this is getting a little creepy! I must have seen this painting before.

ossibly the one I had slept in last night.

Her sister had always wanted to be an ac-
ress, my grandmother said. And when the
me was right, she seized the chance to realize
er dream. What had turned it into a night-
are?

I was there to find out.

The leaves of the dogwood rustled and a
emale cardinal flew to a spot over my head
nd looked at me.

"It's been too long," I said to her. "Too
many years since she died . . . besides, how
o we know she wasn't killed in that fall
ike they said?" It was easier voicing my
oubts to a bird than to my grandmother, who
would have none of them. "It was probably
n accident," I said.

The cardinal turned her back on me and
dropped a foul deposit within an inch of my
new white sneaker, then flew in an arc over
my head.

"Hey, don't take it personally!" I said. "I'm
here, aren't I?" Besides, Plumb-Nelly Tavern
was as good a place to hide as any. But if
anything happened to me here, it was going
to be my grandmother's fault.

"It's Martha — my sister Martha. It must
be . . ." Mama Kate spoke in a questioning
whisper as if she were afraid to say it aloud.

Maybe it hung in my room that summer, or
in the hallway somewhere."

But Bailey shook his head. "It was in the
attic until just about five years ago. Mom
went into a cleaning frenzy after Dad died
and decided to bring it down here. We had
no idea who she was or who painted it until
Aunt Lucy told us."

"It was the only portrait Uncle Chamblee
ever did," Delaney said, setting her empty
glass aside.

The three of them looked at me as if they
expected some logical explanation. I had
none. The silence in the old house was like
a weight, and I felt as if all of it was pressing
on me. "I'm going to bed," I said.

But it was a long time before I fell to sleep
that night. Something was very wrong in this
beautiful place. Did anyone suspect why I
was here?

Chapter Three

A grave is such a lonely place. This one stood apart on a grassy hillside with only a red-tinged dogwood for company. The simple stone marker was probably white when it was placed there in 1936, but time and weather had blotted it gray. Her name, Dahlia Brown, cut in deep block letters above the dates of her birth and death seemed stark, cruel. Irrevocable. My mother's aunt. My grandmother's sister, the one who never came back. She was not yet twenty-one.

"What were you running from, Dahlia Brown?" My words seemed jolting, improper in this quiet place. I looked around to see if anyone was there. I did that a lot lately.

I was simply out for a stroll before breakfast, becoming acquainted again with a setting I had known as a child. No one knew why I was here, and I wanted to keep it that way. Dahlia Brown wasn't the only one who felt the need to hide.

Below me the gold-flecked hills of Fiddler's Glen rolled to meet the craggy North Carolina mountains. It was late September, and the

foliage was just beginning to turn. I p crazy urge to fling out my arms a through the tall grass like the novice t in *The Sound of Music*. And so I did t here would tell? h

The rough stone of the monume n warm to my touch, and a breeze rippl blue-green hillside. Maybe this wasn' a bad place to be buried — when th f came. I hoped mine wouldn't come for a time. Dahlia Brown probably had wish same. From all I had learned about my aunt, she was a bold, outspoken sort, to begin living. She didn't come to this to die.

Behind me the old tavern stood on a w knoll with a low stone wall like a prot arm around it, and looking much as membered. Plumb-Nelly, they called it cause it was located on the old road "p to Morganton and nearly to Wilkesbor had been there since the country was absorbed centuries of secrets into its v clapboard walls. Were some of them aunt's?

Dahlia Brown had come here over years ago to act in the resort's barn the while waiting on tables. She probably stayed in one of the upstairs rooms wl windows opened onto the narrow galler

Her hands shook as she gripped the open magazine on her lap.

"You mean the one who disappeared? Where?" Mama Kate had talked about her missing sister so much, I felt as if she were a part of our lives. Her sepia photograph as a merry-faced toddler sat on my grandmother's mantel. I tossed aside the book I was reading and crossed the room in two steps. The look on her face kind of scared me, and I don't think I've ever heard my grandmother whisper. She isn't the soft-spoken type.

She jabbed the page with her finger. "Says right here: Dahlia Brown. Dahlia. That's what Martha liked to call herself when she was pretending. Hated her name, you know, but your mother is named for her, and so are you, Martha Virginia."

I took the magazine she shoved at me, one of those regional publications with gardening hints, fattening recipes, and folksy stories like "The Night the Bear Cornered Grandpa in the Outhouse." It was turned to the advertisements on the genealogical page.

"There — at the bottom — on the left." Mama Kate sounded as if she'd been chased up a steep hill. Her hand tightened on my arm as I read.

" 'Seek info. relatives Dahlia Brown, 1915–1936, bur. Davenport Family Cemetery.

Contact Bailey Davenport, Plumb-Nelly Tavern, Fiddler's Glen, N.C.' "

"You see — 1936 — that's the very year Martha disappeared, and never a word to any of us!" Mama Kate said. "I knew she wouldn't leave me like that . . . all this time . . . I knew she had to be dead."

But I could tell by my grandmother's voice that she hadn't given up hope entirely — until now.

I read the item again. "I've stayed at Plumb-Nelly Tavern," I said. "It used to be kind of a resort, remember?"

I frowned. "And I remember Bailey Davenport too. He must have been about thirteen that summer. Talked me into doing his chores by bribing me with extra desserts. He spent the whole summer reading Tolkien and I outgrew all my clothes." And he had nearly drowned me, I recalled, when I fell off a foot log into the creek playing follow the leader. It had seemed to take him forever to fish me out with a pine limb.

"Are you going to write?" I asked my grandmother.

"No. I'm going to call." Mama Kate reached for the phone.

Dahlia Brown had died by falling from a bluff near the end of the summer she worked at Plumb-Nelly Tavern, my grandmother learned. It had happened at night, they said. When the owners of the resort were unable to locate her relatives, they buried her at one end of their own family cemetery under the only name they knew: Dahlia Brown.

"But how did they know when she was born?" I asked.

"This young man said she told his aunt — or, rather, his great-aunt — that she would be twenty-one in October. Apparently that's all they had to go on."

Mama Kate still held the receiver against her cheek. She stroked it with her finger. "Martha always had Halloween birthday parties — that is, before we came to live with the aunts."

My grandmother always made a face when she mentioned the aunts who had raised her after her parents died, and she rarely called them by their names, Eleanor and Mabel. Unbending, unsmiling, and unmarried, they had reluctantly taken the two orphan children into their austere home and attempted to mold them into a life-style as rigid as their own. It didn't take.

"Martha hated living with the aunts. And she'd talk back once in a while too, when it got to be too much for her — throw one of her little dramatic tantrums!" She smiled.

"I thought she was the bravest thing in the world. Why, one time she even told Aunt Mabel she wished she'd go to the devil on a greased slide! But she stayed on here for a while after high school and got a job as a clerk in a dry goods store," Mama Kate told me. "The woman who owned the store taught her to sew, and she made me some dresses for school — pretty dresses! A yellow-flowered one and a jade green stripe. The aunts had a fit when I wore them, said they were vulgar and loud." She smiled. "I wore them anyway, just about wore them out."

When her sister had saved enough money, my grandmother said, she planned to go away, find work as an actress. "That's all Martha ever wanted to do," she told me. "We used to make up plays — perform to a make-believe audience. Martha called me Rose, and she was Dahlia. I wasn't much good at it, but Martha was. She could believe she was anybody — and she'd make you believe it too.

"I didn't even cry when she left. I was glad — glad she'd gone somewhere she could laugh, have fun. Martha was beautiful, had that autumn-leaf hair — like yours. Auburn, I guess you'd call it, and eyes as green as a cat's. Yours are darker, Virginia, but you sure do favor her — a lot more than you do your mother or me. And she wasn't afraid of the devil himself!"

Was that why she was wandering too near a dangerous cliff at night? "Was anyone with her when she fell?" I asked. "What was she doing in a place like that?"

My grandmother walked quietly to the bedroom door to check on my grandfather sleeping in the next room. "Well, of course this Davenport fellow — what did you say his name was? Bailey? He wasn't even born until years after Martha was there, but from what he's been told, it was an accident."

"What kind of accident?"

"That's what I'd like to find out." Mama Kate sighed as she sat in the old cherry rocker by the window. It was the same chair she'd sat rocking me when I had chicken pox, and read to me from every fairy tale book on her shelf. The aunts wouldn't allow them, she said, so she made it a point to buy them for her own daughter, my mother.

Absently she tucked a straying lock of gray hair behind her ear. "And why couldn't they find us when Martha died? Let us know? There must have been something — an address book, handbag — something that would identify her. And I'm almost sure she took her birth certificate. She didn't plan to come back, you see."

Mama Kate fumbled in her pocket for the familiar lace-trimmed handkerchief and turned her face away. "I'll send for you, Katie," she said. "When I find a job and a place to stay, I'll send money for a ticket. I promise."

I started to say something, but I saw that she was crying. Katherine Brown Wainwright, known as "the national monument" to two generations of high school students, was *crying*.

"She *promised*. But she never wrote, never called. I was fifteen years old and each day seemed a month long. I checked the mail every day, prayed every night." Mama Kate mopped at her red eyes with a wad of wet linen. "I thought she'd forgotten, that she didn't care anymore."

"Please don't do this to me," I said. "I haven't been programmed for it." I had always felt as if I'd known this mysterious aunt I was supposed to resemble, and whose name I shared. Now I was almost as curious as my grandmother to learn why she never came home. I passed her a box of tissues. "How can you be sure it's her? Maybe it isn't Martha."

"It's Martha. This young man said he'd have his great-aunt get in touch with me when she gets back from Europe. She knew Dahlia

Brown, he says. Maybe she can tell me something. But I don't have to wait to hear it from her. I know it's my sister in that grave."

The state was planning a new highway skirting their property in Fiddler's Glen, Bailey Davenport had explained, and a few yards of it extended into that area of the graveyard where Dahlia Brown was buried.

Neither of us mentioned it to my grandfather, who was recuperating from heart surgery. Mama Kate would quietly arrange to have her sister moved to a place beside their parents in the old churchyard on the outskirts of town.

We sat in her small bright kitchen drinking tea after she had seen to my grandfather for the night. "I can't leave your granddaddy now," Mama Kate said, "or I'd go and look into this myself. But I want to be sure this is Martha — to know the story behind my sister's death. I just don't understand why she never wrote, or told anyone who she was. It wasn't like her. You don't suppose something happened, do you? Something they're not telling me . . ."

"What do you mean?" I reached for a cookie, pretending nonchalance. I didn't like the unsteadiness in her voice or the way she looked at me.

41

"Maybe the fall *wasn't* an accident. Martha *was* headstrong — and probably too candid for her own good . . ." My grandmother met my eyes over the rim of her cup. "You're the only one I can count on, Virginia," she said. "But it might be a good idea if you didn't let on who you are, at least for a little while."

"Why not?" I frowned. "Surely you don't think Aunt Martha was murdered?" My grandmother wasn't the sort to exaggerate. What was the matter with her? I sighed. "And just what do you expect me to do?"

"Oh, for heaven's sake, Virginia, can't you humor me for once? I'd just feel better about it, that's all. I know it's been a long time since it happened . . . you might not find out a thing. But I have to try. Please?"

I couldn't dismiss the urgency in her voice. I had noticed for some time Mama Kate's increasing frailness, her frustration over minor problems that wouldn't even have bothered her the year before. My grandmother was getting old. I didn't have a choice.

And so I was to stay as a guest for a week at Plumb-Nelly, returning to the place I had visited with my parents as a child. And of course I had never heard of Dahlia Brown. I was to keep my eyes and ears open, my grandmother reminded me. And my mouth shut.

Chapter Four

The house was quiet when I returned from my walk, and I hurried upstairs to change my dew-damp shoes before going down for breakfast. It didn't stay quiet long. "But I've cleaned that room!" a voice said outside my door. It was a young voice with the beginning of a whine. I knew the whine would get louder. It did. "I did the best I could. I don't see how you can expect me to do all this stuff in one morning."

"I reckon I musta been dreaming," a woman answered. "You look right pert to me. You got two arms, ain't you? Ain't nothing wrong with your legs. You telling me you don't know how to turn on a vacuum cleaner? There's enough lint under there to fill a gunnysack. And look at that bed, Sheri Griffin! Looks like somebody's been dancing on it."

The girl giggled. "Maybe they have."

I looked at the clock on the mantel. It was already after eight. Sunlight streaked across a rose-patterned rug; dark, polished floor-boards; and glinted off the beveled mirror above a washstand that would sell for a for-

43

tune in an antiques shop. It looked very much at home here with the walnut four-poster and delicate floral wallpaper.

I splashed water on my face, smoothed my hair, and started downstairs, hoping I wasn't too late for breakfast. In a room at the far end of the hall a vacuum cleaner growled angrily, and in the foyer below, a tall, large-boned woman with a ruddy face whisked a dustcloth over a gilt-framed picture. She turned when she saw me. "Well, good morning! You must be the new one — and I'll bet you're hungry. I've kept some sausage and biscuits warm for you, and there's juice and cereal on the sideboard. Just help yourself." She smiled, revealing one gold tooth. "Bailey told me you come here when you was just a little thing. Welcome back. I'm Ethelene. Ethelene Cleveland. I'm the cook and house-keeper — of sorts."

I recognized her voice. She was the woman who had been about to jerk a knot in Sheri for sloppy housekeeping. I took the hand she offered. It was freckled and rough; evidently Ethelene didn't believe in wearing rubber gloves. I thanked her and introduced myself. It was all I could do to stand there and be polite. I had smelled the sausage, and to hell with calories! And I needed coffee in the worst way. "Looks like you have your

44

work cut out for you," I said. "How many rooms are there here?"

"Too many!" She took a swipe at the stair railing and rubbed briskly at the massive carved newel post. "But you and Mrs. Stafford-Smith are the only overnights right now. Couple in that front room left just after breakfast, and Mrs. Abernathy's not due till tomorrow. She always stays here when she visits her daughter. All them grandchildren makes her nervous, you know."

I nodded, backing toward the dining room. If I needed information about anything at Plumb-Nelly, I knew where to come.

The house was quiet as I ate at a small table by the window. At the far end of the lawn Rob Quillian trimmed weeds away from the wall and piled them in a wheelbarrow. As I finished my second cup of coffee I heard Delaney speak briefly to Mrs. Cleveland before going out the back way, her heels making stacatto taps on the old oak floors. She zoomed past my window behind the wheel of a modest blue sedan, blowing the horn at Rob on her way out. I was kind of surprised. I expected Delaney to drive something expensive and flashy. Delaney Davenport must be at least in her early thirties. For some reason, I thought she would have pursued some glamorous career, or at least married a handsome millionaire by now. I wondered why she was still at Plumb-Nelly.

Ethelene Cleveland appeared at my elbow and poured me another cup of coffee which I didn't need but drank anyway. "That girl's gonna kill herself one of these days, driving like that," she said with a sigh. "That curve down there's done taken poor Charlotte Millsap. You'd think folks would learn, wouldn't you?"

I said I would and thanked her for my breakfast. But I knew she wasn't through.

"Trying her luck with a gift shop, Delaney is — out there next to Otto's store. Don't know what she thinks she'll sell in there — or who to, for that matter. We don't get that many folks through here." She leaned heavily on the back of a chair and studied the table-cloth. "Seems she don't know what to do with herself since she come home last year."

I took the bait. "Home from where?"

"Some kind of job out in California; studied drawing out there, painting — that kind of thing. Well, I could've told her you can't make no living out of that. Then what does she do? Ups and marries this man she hadn't known more than a few weeks." Mrs. Cleveland shifted her weight and moaned. "You know the type: looks like some kind of movie star, but poor as Job's turkey. I reckon he thought she had money, and she thought he could get her in to meet the right people." She looked around to see if anyone was listening, then dropped her voice. "The only thing that man got her into was debt. 'Course I'll have to hand it to her, she stuck it out for almost two years — but by then he'd already spent all she had and more."

Ethelene frowned as we heard Sheri — or somebody — clattering down the steps with the vacuum cleaner. "I'd better go see what that girl's up to," she said, shaking her head. "I have to go right behind her — and me with these bad feet. Can't get a shoe to fit a narrow foot like mine." She limped away, muttering, and I grabbed the chance to escape before she could ply me with more food, remembering what had happened the last time I stayed here.

The sheet music was still stacked on the piano, where we had left it the night before, and I was tempted to sit down and play, but I didn't want to call attention to myself. What if the tyrannical Mrs. Stafford-Smith was still in a card-playing mood?

Someone had arranged a few pink roses in a silver bud vase on the table beside the fireplace, and I thought it made a fitting tribute

47

to the painting that hung above it. The girl in the swing looked young and fresh like the roses, and she wore a slight smile as if she knew that life was good, and that this was only the beginning. Her simple dress was a splash of pastel colors with a full skirt that billowed about her, and she held an armful of daisies on her lap. Around her neck was the dainty coral necklace my grandmother had told me about. It had belonged to her mother.

"Pretty thing, ain't she?" Ethelene said behind me. "Hair about the same color as yours." She squinted at me. "Shoot, she could pretty near pass for your sister . . . 'course this might not look a thing like her. You can't tell nothing about a painting."

"Bailey said she died soon after this was painted," I said. "Fell from a cliff, or something."

Ethelene folded her arms and nodded. "Some say she heard the fiddle."

"What fiddle?"

"Lucifer's fiddle. At least that's what we've always called it." Ethelene lowered the lid over the piano keys and made a pass at dusting around the music. "We've always had our share of fiddlers here — that's where the place gets its name — but back during the War Between the States there was a fellow lived about a mile from here they say could outfiddle them all: Willie Hugh Jordan. Man could play a dead mule into plowing, folks said."

Ethelene sat on the piano bench and spread her blue gingham skirt as if she were about to play, but she only rubbed her worn hands over the polished wood. "He fell in love with a girl named Jean McCorey," she said, looking up at me. "They planned a wedding as soon as the war was over, and when he went riding off on his horse Biscuit to fight for the Confederacy, Willie Hugh promised he'd come back playing that fiddle. 'When you hear "Jeanie with the Light Brown Hair," ' he said, 'it'll be me coming down the road to meet you.' And sure enough, after about a year Jean McCorey woke up one night when the moon was as bright as day, tossed a blanket around her, and ran out across that field just the other side of Plumb-Nelly to meet her fiddling lover. The next morning they found her body at the bottom of that ravine — same place where that Dahlia Brown ended up almost seventy-five years later."

I smiled. I loved a good ghost story too. "How do they know she heard it?"

From the look I got, I knew I had just slipped a couple of rungs in Ethelene's opinion. "Her own ma heard it! Little brother too. Hoofbeats coming faster, closer. And then that music. Said it was as clear as if he'd been riding right through that meadow. A few weeks later they got word Willie Hugh had been killed that very afternoon."

She rose wearily and stood looking at the girl in the painting. "It wasn't her sweetheart that lured Jean McCorey to her death, it was the devil himself. And from what they say about the way this one died, it wouldn't surprise me none if she went the same way." The big woman nodded solemnly. "That poor girl heard Lucifer's fiddle."

I turned away from the picture. The ghost story had suddenly lost its appeal. "What makes you think that?" I asked.

Ethelene sighed. "Because she'd heard it before. At least, that's what they said."

I frowned. "Who said?"

"Well, some of the people who worked here then — and Lucy Whitworth too. They were right good friends, you know."

"Did anybody else hear it?"

Ethelene gave me a gold-toothed grin. "Honey, believe it or not, I was just a shirt-tailed lap youngun about then. You'll have to ask them that knows." And she snatched up her dust rag and disappeared into the kitchen.

A flash of color caught my eye as Rob Quillian, wearing a red plaid shirt, trundled a load of straw past the window, and I was glad to be distracted by something so commonplace. It brought me back to the present and to reality. Briefly. I looked again. Rob had weeded his way along the old stone wall to the big, square columns at the entrance, and there, wearing an open khaki jacket and peering at the tavern through a camera stood the very person I'd been trying to avoid.

I didn't expect my reaction. The sight of the man made me physically ill. Where could I hide now? It was too late to run. The eerie tale Ethelene had told me seemed almost trifling compared to the revulsion I felt. How had Gideon Foster known to find me here?

Chapter Five

From the upstairs hallway I heard the distinctive tapping of Mrs. Stafford-Smith's ebony cane, and could almost see her there, playing cards in hand, waiting to ensnare her unwilling victims — just like a big black widow. I would have to pass her on the stairs in order to get to my room.

I looked for a convenient exit. Was Gideon Foster on his way to the house? I hadn't heard a car. At the sound of the first footstep on the porch I would take refuge in the kitchen — hide in the pantry if necessary. Quickly I risked another glance out the window and almost laughed out loud in relief. The photographer in the khaki jacket was posing what looked like a family group against a cluster of dogwoods. He was of similar build and coloring as Gideon, but on second look I could see the receding hairline and bare upper lip.

"Sorry, I didn't know anybody was in here. I was going to run the sweeper." A young girl stood in the doorway trailing the long cord of the vacuum cleaner, and even in the plain blue dress and apron she was pretty in an unfinished sort of way. She would have been just as pretty without the glittery eye shadow and pale pink lipstick; she looked about seventeen. "I can come back later," she said, glancing toward the closed kitchen door. "Long as I get it done before noon."

I stiffened at the ominous sound of Eugenia descending the stairs. "No, that's all right. I think I'll just step out the back way. You go right ahead."

The girl giggled as she plugged in the sweeper. "I won't tell," she said.

The morning air was brisk, even in sunlight, and I was glad I had thought to wear a sweater as I wandered past the pecan grove behind the house and through the wrought iron gates to the old family cemetery where I had walked earlier. And almost without thinking I stood again at my great-aunt's grave. Beautiful view, but a bit depressing. What in the world was the matter with me? I hadn't meant to come here.

As I turned to go, it became unnaturally quiet, even for such a place. Not a bird sang, and I knew without seeing that someone was standing behind me.

But when I looked, all I saw was a faint blur near a grave at the end of a row. I had experienced that peculiar feeling before: you think you see something out of the corner of your eye, yet when you look, there's nothing there. Fool's phantoms, Mama Kate calls them. If anyone had been standing there, it would have been impossible for them to disappear so quickly; yet I walked slowly up the hill, feeling a little embarrassed for thinking what I was thinking.

The square marble slab belonged to no one I'd ever heard of: James Curtis Davenport had died at the age of seventy-four in 1922. The only thing that set his stone apart was the Masonic emblem carved above his name.

I stood there feeling like a complete idiot when it happened again: the same uncanny awareness of someone there, followed by a spooky little vanishing act. This time, about halfway up the hillside, I discovered the grave of Edward Penfield. He was buried there in 1948, and he, too, was a member of the Masonic Order.

What did it mean? Once more I found myself at the grave of Dahlia Brown. Someone — or something — had led me to those stones. The men had lived and died at different times, different ages. What could they possibly have to do with my aunt's death? Was the person responsible for her fall a member of the Masons? What was she trying to tell me?

Had I been dreaming? Maybe I should pinch

myself. But I knew I hadn't imagined it. I shook my head. Face it, Ginger: This is your day to see phantoms! The man with the camera had looked so much like someone I knew, I would have wagered an entire cherry cheesecake on it. For a few horrible minutes I thought Gideon Foster had followed me here. I still had what felt like a large rock in my throat from what I had only imagined I'd seen earlier. "I can't go back," I said aloud. "Not as long as he's there."

Dry leaves rustled behind me, and I turned to see Bailey Davenport with his hands deep in his pockets and a puzzled smile on his face. "Go back where?" he said.

I groaned. Had he seen me running from grave to grave like a participant in some macabre game? But if he was aware of anything unusual, he didn't mention it.

"You weren't supposed to hear that," I said. "What are you doing here anyway? Don't you know better than to sneak up on somebody in a graveyard? You scared me half to death."

"Sorry," Bailey said, but he didn't look it. "I saw you passing my study window and followed you here." He looked at the lonely gravestone. "I see you've found her — the girl in the swing." He frowned. "Seems sort of a shame to move her now."

We walked together through the tall grass to a sun-warm rock on the hillside, and Bailey pulled me down beside him. "Now, tell me where you can't go — and why."

I looked across at the knoll of hardwoods, where a lone hawk circled, then disappeared. "Home," I said. "Shell City. There's someone there who makes me feel uneasy. Well, more than uneasy — just plain scared."

"Is that why you came here — alone?"

"Partly. I just knew I had to get away — for a while at least. I had some vacation time coming and a little money saved, but now I know it's going to take longer than I thought." I told Bailey about seeing the man with the camera and how it had affected me.

He looked at me for a minute. "Can you tell me about it?" he said finally.

I had dated Gideon for about a year and a half, I told Bailey, before I realized his jealous obsession. We met at the newspaper where I worked and where he was a part-time photographer. Gideon worked free-lance and supplemented his spasmodic income by supplying photos for several papers in the area. He was tall and good-looking, an excellent dancer, engaging conversationalist, and could have served as a model for a Chippendale's calendar. Also, I liked being with him. For a while.

Bailey watched a squirrel scampering along the limbs of a crimson-hued sweet gum. "And then what happened?"

"I think it was when he bought the Jaguar — a bright red one, and it drove like a dream. It was fun at first, but that's all he could talk about. Gideon seemed to be consumed by the power it gave him, and it soon became apparent that power extended to me."

Bailey stared silently ahead, waiting for me to go on, and I shifted my position on the hard rock. "We each seemed to care about the other," I said, "but neither of us had spoken about a commitment. I wasn't ready, and I didn't think Gideon was either. Gradually he seemed to think of me as a possession — just like the car. I didn't understand it, but I knew I didn't like it. And when I tried to discuss it, Gideon grew erratic — almost hostile." I shrugged. "I'm afraid I didn't handle it very well."

"What did you do?" Bailey asked.

"I told him to take a hike. And then I thanked my lucky stars I'd seen what he was like before things went any further." I laughed. "I would've burned incense if I were into that sort of thing."

"I take it this Gideon couldn't take rejection."

"Not only that, but he collected photographs — evidence, he called it — of my 'unfaithfulness.' "

Bailey shaded his eyes from the sun. "What do you mean?"

"Well, sometimes while we were still seeing each other I would go out with friends — girlfriends mostly, or I'd have to go to a meeting. And there were times when I just preferred staying at home. Gideon practically accused me of carrying on some clandestine affair, and later I found out he'd followed me. Can you believe it? He actually checked up on me — even had the pictures to prove it!"

"What kind of pictures?" Bailey asked, pulling me to my feet.

"Just innocent photographs of me standing next to some man in a parking lot. We had just come from a planning session for the annual spring festival. I was in charge of publicity. And there were a couple of photos of me beside a friend's pool; he really got hot about that because her brother was with me. He was fourteen."

"My God! The man must be paranoid." Bailey held back a low-hanging limb as we walked beneath it.

"More than that, I'm afraid. A couple of the pictures were taken with a zoom lens through my bedroom window. It was broad daylight and I was dressing for work. I had no idea anyone could see inside — or would even want to."

"He *showed* you these photographs?"

"No, not those. They were in a folder in his car. We were on our way to lunch one day in a last-ditch effort to make peace, and I saw them while he was in the post office mailing some prints."

Bailey put his hand on my arm as we walked through the blotted green shade of the pecan grove. "What did you do? Didn't you say anything?"

"Of course. I tore up the pictures and accused him of being a Peeping Tom and worse. He only laughed, said he still had the negatives." I stopped for a minute, forced myself to speak calmly. "I just left him standing there. I never saw him again . . . but I knew he was watching. And then there were the phone calls with nobody on the other end."

"I suppose you've reported all this to the police."

"Naturally, and they said they'd keep an eye on him, but they can't do a thing unless he actually does something. I guess they have their hands full with drug pushers and people killing one another."

"What about your family?" Bailey asked.

I shrugged. "Mom's concerned, of course, but to tell you the truth, I'm sure she thinks

I'm exaggerating. It was my stepfather who suggested I go away for a while. Since I work for his newspaper, I don't have to worry about job security — still, this money won't last forever. I can't stay away indefinitely."

"Does anyone know where you are?"

"Well, yes. My grandmother knows, and Mom and Haynes — Haynes Reinhold, my stepfather. And they've promised not to tell. I feel like a secret agent or something with all this cloak-and-dagger stuff, but I still get the jitters whenever I think about it. I know Gideon. If he wants to find me, he will." The words had slipped out before I knew it, and I wanted to take them back, erase them, but I knew what I had said was true.

Bailey didn't speak until we reached the house, where he paused at the back steps. "I hope you won't take this the wrong way, Ginger, but if you'd like to stay on here for a while, we could use the extra help. Now that Delaney's opened that shop, she doesn't seem to have enough hours in the day. It's not too bad during the week, but Ethelene and Sheri just can't handle the weekends alone." He smiled. "We can't pay much, but room and board is free, and I couldn't help but notice how great you and Rob sounded together last night. It couldn't hurt business if you did that more often; and then if things pick up, we'll be in a position to offer a little more."

Bailey stepped back and looked at me. "Well, what do you say?"

I didn't know what to say. It sounded almost too good to be true, yet for some reason I hesitated. "Let me think about it," I said as we went up the steps together. "Can I let you know later?"

Bailey held the door for me. "Take your time . . . and you might want to talk with my uncle Chamblee. He's co-owner of the local weekly — kind of getting along in years now, but he likes to keep his hand in. They could probably use a boost in their advertising sales, if you're interested."

I nodded. "Thanks, I'll keep it in mind," I said. But Bailey had already disappeared behind the massive door of his study. I found myself wondering if he belonged to the Masons.

Eugenia waited for me in the front parlor, where she sat enthroned by the door. "I've reserved us a table for lunch," she said. "This place fills up so fast, they'll try to squeeze you in with every Tom, Dick, and Harry if you'll let them."

She gave me what would probably pass for a smile and patted my hand. She had the longest, reddest fingernails I'd ever seen.

They looked as if they could draw blood. I wondered if they were real.

"Why, thank you, Mrs. Stafford-Smith, but you really —"

"Eugenia. I told you to call me Eugenia! And be sure to meet me here at one. We have a lot to talk about." She went back to her crossword puzzle. I was dismissed.

I was also snared. Skewered. Doomed. And stupid. I should have been more careful.

But lunch turned out to be an interesting affair. Rob joined us, as did Delaney, along with a nice-looking man who turned out to be the new doctor and an obvious admirer of Delaney's. Sam Molloy could hardly take his eyes from her during the meal, but Delaney wasn't interested, or didn't seem to be.

"The doctor's been married," Eugenia told me later when the two of us were alone. "And he has custody of the children. Three of them — oldest is seven."

"Oh," I said. "Well, he seems very nice. Good-looking too."

She gave her odd little grimace. "But no money. Can you see Delaney Davenport wiping runny noses? Joining the P.T.A.?" She sniffed. "Men are such fools sometimes! Can't see beyond the ends of their noses."

I agreed. It was odd how often Eugenia and

I thought alike. I wondered how long it would be before I became peculiar and started to wear funny clothes.

Ethelene had served up a fine bean soup made with last night's ham bone, and I devoured every spoonful, along with hot corn muffins and cole slaw. When Sheri came around with a plate of pound cake, I made my excuses and fled. Delaney had said her uncle Chamblee usually dropped by the newspaper office for an hour or so in the afternoon, so I drove the three miles into Fiddler's Glen hoping to find him.

"Just missed him," the woman at the front desk told me. "This is one of his 'landscape' days — light's just right, he says."

My confusion must have been evident, because she smiled. "Sorry, I forget people who aren't from around here wouldn't know. Mr. Davenport's an artist, does landscapes — oils mostly. It's just a hobby, of course, but since he's more or less passed *The Bugle* over to the Cuthberts, he has more time to paint."

I remembered now; Chamblee Davenport was the one who painted that portrait of Dahlia Brown. Now I wanted to talk with him more than ever. "Do you know when he'll be back?" I asked.

She shook her head. "No tellin'. But if

you're staying at the tavern, he'll be there for supper. He's a Wednesday night regular." The woman smiled. "Ethelene always has fruit cobbler — his favorite, you know."

I didn't know and didn't really care, but I thanked her and left to do some shopping in Morganton. If I planned to stay at Plumb-Nelly, I would have to have a few more necessities.

It was twilight by the time I turned through the sturdy stone columns and drove up the long curving drive to the tavern, and for a brief minute I felt as if I were coming home. Dim lights shone from the parlor and a couple of people rocked on the downstairs porch, waiting comfortably for their supper. Then as I drew nearer I heard it: the squeaking of a swing, and it seemed to come from the gallery above.

It was a good thing no one was behind me, because I stopped dead in the middle of the driveway. The red-haired girl in the painting, full skirts flying, smiled down at me and waved. Then she touched the coral necklace at her throat and promptly disappeared.

Chapter Six

Several people spoke to me as I walked up the steps and into the house. I don't know who they were. I don't think I even acknowledged them as I hurried upstairs. Double doors at the end of the hall opened onto the upper gallery, but I knew before I pushed them ajar that the girl in the swing wouldn't be there. And I was right. The porch was deserted. A wooden-slatted swing hung motionless at one end. The wrong end.

A large Boston fern on a wrought iron stand stood beside a rocking chair on the opposite side, where I had seen the girl in the wicker swing — just like the one in the painting. I walked over and looked at the ceiling. Two metal eyelets painted gray like the woodwork were fastened about four feet apart, and I knew they had once supported a swing.

I looked around me. No one could move furniture so quickly. Could I have imagined what I saw? Yet I knew I had seen her before on several occasions when I was here as a child. I drew my sweater closer to me as I started inside, and that was when I saw it. A lone daisy lay beneath the fern stand as if it had been dropped there. I picked it up and ran the blossom through my fingers, plucking at a petal. The flower was real; it was fresh. I could smell it. It was also out of season. Dahlia Brown was here, had never left Plumb-Nelly Tavern. What did she want of me?

I put the daisy in a water glass in my room. Should I mention this to someone? But who? Mama Kate had her hands full with my grandfather's illness. Besides, she probably wouldn't believe me. Bailey Davenport? No. Then I would have to reveal my identity, and for now I agreed with my grandmother; no one should know I was related to Dahlia Brown.

But keeping this secret was becoming increasingly difficult as I found out during dinner. Again I was seated at the long table Eugenia scorned, this time across from Chamblee Davenport. "Since you missed him at *The Bugle*," Bailey said, "I thought you might like the opportunity to talk."

Still handsome at almost eighty, Bailey's uncle had the same clear-cut features and easy grace as his great-niece and -nephew. But there was a gentle reserve about him that the younger Davenports lacked, a benign tolerance, as if he had learned to deal with life on its own terms and had endured in spite of it. Chamblee Davenport was a survivor. From time to time I found him looking at me, and wondered how long it would take him to ask the inevitable question. After all, he had painted Dahlia Brown, had been on intimate terms with her face: a face much like my own.

Finally, over the fruit cup, he raised pensive blue eyes to mine. "I once knew someone very much like you," he said, toying with a twist of lime. "Looking at you, I feel as if fifty years had vanished in a few seconds." Chamblee Davenport dropped the fruit peeling onto his salad plate and slowly smoothed his napkin. "More than fifty years," he added softly.

Delaney frowned. "The girl in the painting. You do look like her, you know. Maybe she's a relative."

I took a sip of water. It took a long time going down. "I guess it's because we share the same coloring." And speaking of coloring, was my face as red as it felt? "This pineapple is wonderful," I said, and stuffed a spoonful into my mouth.

"Dahlia never spoke of her relatives," he said. "Except for a younger sister — Rose, she called her."

"Did Bailey tell you he finally got in touch with her about moving the grave?" Delaney asked. "Only her name isn't Rose. They're having Dahlia's body reinterred in a few weeks, I think."

Her uncle frowned. "Not a suitable topic for the table, Delaney." He smiled at me. "My niece tells me you were a guest here once before. I believe I had dinner with your parents a few times. Your father was a professor at State? Taught political science?"

I nodded, delighted at his excellent memory. "And history. They made him department head just a couple of years before he died."

He frowned. "Oh? And when was this?"

"When I was thirteen. It was a sailing accident." We had rented a cottage on the coast that summer — our last summer together.

I sensed someone behind me and looked up to see Ethelene standing there with a troubled face. "Bless your heart," she said, and swooped my dish away, replacing it with trout almondine.

I smiled. "Anyway, my mother sold real estate for a while, and then when I was sixteen she married Haynes Reinhold. He's publisher of *The Shell City Dispatch* down close to Tampa."

"Ginger's in advertising sales," Bailey

added, breaking open a steaming yeast roll. He glanced up. "She just might be interested in selling some space for you."

"Oh?" His uncle looked at me. "How long are you going to be here? We're in between ad managers right now, and I'm too darned old to fool with it. Would you really be interested in giving us a hand?" He took a swallow of coffee and regarded me with his wise old eyes. "Just until we can get somebody else."

I laughed. "Are you sure you really want me?"

Chamblee Davenport concentrated on his fish. "If we didn't, I wouldn't ask you," he said. "Of course you realize the pay is next to pathetic."

"How can I possibly turn down an offer like that?" I said. "I accept."

My new employer shook my hand over the bread basket. "Good. Now please pass the preserves."

The next day I moved into my new room. "This really isn't necessary," Bailey insisted, following me down the narrow back hallway. "Stay where you are through the weekend at least. We don't expect that many guests."

I shoved open my door with one knee and dumped an armload of clothing on the narrow spool bed. "I don't want to get spoiled," I said, checking the storage space under the window seat. "Besides, it's cozy here. I like it." And I did. The room was small, but the white paneled walls and blue gingham curtains gave it an airy charm, and the calico Agnes curled up immediately on the worn rag rug.

Bailey and I had agreed that I would fill in for Delaney at the tavern on weekends and whenever else I could, and Rob and I would try to work up some sort of musical agenda to entertain at least a few nights a week. That would leave most of my weekdays free to see if I could pull in some ads for *The Bugle*.

Bailey shook his head and left me there to return a few minutes later with my overstuffed luggage. "Suit yourself," he said, and set it on the floor with a thud.

Rob Quillian popped his head in the doorway and made a face at the cat. "Good. I see you've inherited this horrible animal. Now maybe she'll leave me alone." He shoved my clothing aside and plopped on the bed. "Anyway, welcome to the back row. My room's two doors down."

"Who's on either side of me?" I asked.

"Well, nobody right now," Bailey said. "Sheri and Ethelene usually go home every night, but they'll sometimes stay over in bad

70

weather. And Mercer Belle Abernathy usually asks for that end one; it has a private bath." He looked at his watch. "She should be chugging in sometime this afternoon."

Rob grinned. "And you'll know it the minute she steps inside."

I didn't ask how. I didn't want to know. Did normal people *ever* stay at Plumb-Nelly?

Rob slowly unfolded his long frame and walked to the window in two steps. "Looks like rain; glad I got that grass planted out front. When you're ready to come downstairs, let me know, and we'll go over some of that music."

I nodded, urging both of them out the door. There was barely room for one person and a cat. Hurriedly I tossed my meager supply of cosmetics in the top drawer of the pine dresser and inhaled a musty floral smell. Obviously a previous tenant had left behind a sachet. I ran my hand along the paper-lined interior but found nothing.

A streak of color rushed by my feet as the cat leapt to the window seat, where she arched her back and kneaded the paisley cushion until I was afraid it would tear.

"What's the matter with you, Agnes? Leave that cushion alone!" I deposited her on the floor, where she darted under the bed, leaving me to unpack in peace. I had almost forgotten about her when, almost an hour later, she dashed past me as I opened the door and stalked into Rob's room down the hall. I found her there chewing on a discarded sock.

"This beast is neurotic," Rob said, retrieving his sock. "And thoroughly untrustworthy. You never know where you stand."

"I take it you don't like cats."

"Never found one to measure up to Uncle Barney." Rob handed me a framed picture from a small desk in the corner. It was a photograph of a dog, an English bulldog. "Uncle Barney," he said. "Best friend I ever had. Almost sixteen when he died last year."

I made some kind of noise that was meant to be sympathetic and turned away. It was the ugliest dog I had ever seen and I was afraid I was going to laugh. How perfectly horrible of me! Here he was baring his soul and I was acting like an insensitive clod.

"That's okay. Go ahead and laugh," Rob said. "Uncle Barney affects people that way. Ugly son of a bitch, wasn't he?"

I could only nod. Agnes purred around my feet and I stooped to scratch her neck. Only minutes ago she had hidden from me beneath the bed, and now she wanted to be best friends.

Later that night she followed me meekly into my room and watched from the foot of my bed while I wrote to Mama Kate explaining that I would be staying longer at Plumb-Nelly. It was a short letter because I was tired and the plump white pillows looked inviting. Earlier Rob had talked me into accompanying him on my flute, and I think we must have gone through every piece of music I brought with me, but the guests seemed to enjoy it, especially the rotund Mrs. Abernathy, who fell asleep in her chair until she woke herself with her own snoring. I giggled as I heard her snorting blast at the end of the hall, then pulled the covers over my ears to block out the noise.

That was all I heard until much later, when the cat dug her claws into my leg and bounded to the floor, screeching to get out. "I've had it with you," I told her, jerking open the door. "Find yourself another roommate." Agnes took off down the dark hall and I tumbled back into bed to huddle beneath the warm quilt. Stupid cat! I was beginning to feel partial to Uncle Barney myself. What if I couldn't get back to sleep? I looked at the clock. It was after five, and although it was still dark, morning had begun to claim her own and I could distinguish objects in the small room. Books stacked on the window seat, my robe thrown over the back of a chair, the vase of daisies on the dresser.

I lay there like a piece of wood, staring at the furniture across from me. *There had been no vase of flowers there before I went to bed.* Had there? Or maybe I just hadn't noticed. Was I that tired?

Timidly I reached for the light beside my bed and was immediately reassured. I must have imagined seeing the arrangement. There were no flowers on the dresser. I closed my eyes and opened them. The reflection of the daisies was still in the mirror, and as I watched it began to fade until the image was gone.

Chapter Seven

Eugenia skewered me over the breakfast table with her dark, probing eyes. "I suggest you take a nap this morning, Virginia. You don't look well at all. Is something bothering you?" She leaned forward and peered at me. "You're not anemic, are you?"

"I guess it's getting used to a different bed," I said, putting too much pepper on my scrambled eggs. "I didn't get a lot of sleep last night."

She scowled. "I'll have Bailey change your mattress, then. There's no excuse for that."

"No, no, it's not the mattress. The mattress is fine. Haven't you ever been so tired you couldn't get to sleep?" I buttered a muffin and smiled at her. "I'll try to rest this afternoon or turn in early tonight." I couldn't, of course. I had promised to help Ethelene in the kitchen today, and Rob Quillian and I were to entertain for an hour or so during dinner, but I didn't dare confess this to Eugenia and have her confront Bailey Davenport. After all, I was no longer a paying guest at Plumb-Nelly Tavern. Besides, Eugenia tended to exaggerate. I couldn't possibly look as awful as I felt.

"My Lord! What in the world's the matter with you? You look like you've been rode hard and put up wet." Ethelene Cleveland sat at the kitchen table making out her grocery list, her stocking feet propped on the rung of the chair. A pair of black oxfords, very shiny and very narrow, sat neatly beside her.

I leaned over her shoulder. "The cat woke me in the middle of the night and I couldn't get back to sleep. Do you want white onions or yellow? Is that self-rising flour or plain?"

"Yellow," she said. "Plain. How do you like your new room?"

"It's small but comfortable, and the furniture's really pretty. Some of those pieces look like antiques. Makes you wonder about all the people who've stayed there, what they were like."

I could tell by the look on her face that Ethelene didn't share such strange notions. "Huh! Can't hardly get the sweeper in them little bitty rooms, and that old rag rug needs to be thrown out, if you ask me."

I took the grocery list from her and sat beside her. "I'll bet someone from that group of actors stayed in there," I said. "Slept in that very bed."

"What actors?"

"You know; the ones who were here when the barn was a theater. Maybe the girl in the painting. She could have, you know."

"I reckon." Ethelene snatched the list from me and added *2 boxes dark brown sugar* in firm, round handwriting.

"Unless," I said, "they had rooms out in the barn."

She shrugged. "Lucy would know, I guess. You'll have to ask her when she gets back."

I looked up. "When do think that will be?"

"Could be next week; could be next month. I think she went over there just to get away from all them politics. Lucy don't hold too much with all that carryin'-on." And Ethelene padded over to stick her head into the big white refrigerator. "Better add a half gallon of buttermilk to that," she said.

I nodded. "What politics?"

"Why, the governor's race! Her son's running for lieutenant governor, didn't you know?"

"Lucy Whitworth's son? Of course — Woodrow Whitworth! Why hadn't I connected the names?" I frowned. "Wonder why his dad never mentioned it?" I had sat with

Kirby Whitworth during dinner only a few nights before and I couldn't remember him saying a thing about it.

" 'Cause everybody's sick of hearing it, I reckon. That Kirby can run even a good thing into the ground. If he has his way about it, that boy will be president of the United States whether he wants to or not." Ethelene rinsed a good-sized hen and patted it dry with a wad of paper towels.

"Doesn't he want to run for office?"

"Who knows? Wants what his daddy wants, if you ask me. Kirby Whitworth owned a whole bunch of businesses here before he retired — made a lot of money too — but Woodrow didn't seem to care about that. He took more after his uncle Chamblee. And his mama was perfectly satisfied when Woodrow got out of college and decided to go to work for Chamblee. Took that newspaper course, you know — the one that teaches you how to do all that stuff. But now he's into this politicking!"

I smiled. "Wonder what made him change his mind."

"Brainwashed, that's what. Just plain brainwashed." Ethelene glanced at the clock. "Guess you'd better get going if I'm to make them *quiches* for lunch."

She pronounced the word so that it rhymed

with *peaches,* and I was glad of an excuse to leave before she noticed my reaction. But I didn't get far.

"Hold on a minute!" Ethelene yelled at me from the back door. "Don't let that Otto Millsap sell you any of them old rotten onions. I got some in there last week, smelled up my pantry so bad I had to throw the whole bag out . . . and if you see that Rob, tell him this old sink's leaking again!"

I almost ran into Bailey Davenport on my way to the car. "I hear you need a new mattress," he said, walking with me to the parking area.

I groaned. Eugenia! "There's not a thing wrong with my mattress," I assured him. "And I love that pretty old spool bed. Has it always been in there?"

"As far as I know, that room hasn't been changed for years — except for the quilt and curtains. Mother added those before she remarried and moved to Maine." Bailey opened the door for me on the driver's side of the car. "No, wait a minute. I take that back. The dresser in there was some kind of hideous metal thing. We got rid of that and hauled this one down from the attic." He grinned. "Had to put two coats of wax on it. No telling how long it had been up there."

I smiled as I drove away. I knew. And Dahlia Brown knew as well. I wanted to share my story with somebody else, but no one would believe me. I hardly believed it myself.

Grace Millsap looked up at me with bulging blue eyes. "Is this quiche made with skim milk? I have to watch my cholesterol, you know; and that looks like ham in there to me." She sucked in her breath through her thin little nose. "Seems like that Ethelene can't make anything that's not fattening."

The woman couldn't have weighed more than a hundred pounds, and a fourth of that was in the nest of tight curls she wore. "I can bring you the tuna salad," I suggested. "Or the fruit plate." I tried not to look at the table across from her, where Eugenia sat with Mercer Belle Abernathy ladling muscadine preserves on buttered biscuits.

Grace Millsap cleared her slender throat. "Nothing really appeals to me since I had that virus last month. Awful cramps, and couldn't hold a thing on my stomach for over a week. Why, Dr. Molloy swears he didn't know how I —"

Behind her, Eugenia's dark brows arched as she tapped a spoon on her water goblet. "Perhaps you would like to announce that to the rest of the diners, Grace. Then we could all lose our appetites," she said in a loud voice.

Mrs. Millsap gripped her fork like a dagger and turned the color of the rosy camellia she wore pinned to her sweater. "Well, really, Eugenia —"

"It wouldn't do you a bit of harm to put on a little weight, fill out some of those angles," Eugenia went on. "Why, you might even develop a bosom — but then, I guess it's too late to worry about that."

Mrs. Abernathy giggled into her napkin. "Oh, Eugenia!"

But Grace Millsap wasn't amused. "You are a coarse woman, Eugenia," she said, letting each word fall like a brick. "I don't care if you do have three last names!"

Mrs. T.S.S. looked thunderous. "And if it hadn't been for you, you silly little woman, my poor Charlotte would still be alive!"

I looked around for help. There wasn't any, of course. "I'll get some coffee," I said, scurrying for the pot. When I came back, Eugenia and her cohort had left, and Mrs. Millsap had returned her fork to its accustomed place. "I believe I'll just have a salad," she said, staring at me with a familiar glint. "You look like somebody." Her frown told me it was someone she disapproved of. And I knew who that was.

"Someone I used to know . . ." She tapped on the table with blunt fingertips.

I poured her coffee, averting my face. It would come to her in time.

It did. "Why, it's that actress! The one in the painting in there — Dahlia something-or-other."

"Must be the hair," I said, taking away the rejected quiche. "Several people have mentioned it."

"Now, there's one you wouldn't want to imitate," the woman said. "No better than she ought to be, let me tell you. Flirted with anything in pants — and that's not all she did either, from what I've heard tell!" Her mouth tightened. "Why, do you know what she said to me once? 'Loosen up, Grace, and have some fun. You act like you've got a corn cob up your ass!' Of course, I wasn't real surprised at her talking like that — seeing as how she behaved."

I backed away from her, my fingers gripping the handle of the pot, and clenched my teeth so hard my jaw hurt. I didn't know whether to laugh or hit her over the head. I was at least two tables away when I heard her shrill cry and saw the steaming coffee from her overturned cup trickle into her lap.

"Oh, dear Lord, I'm scalded! Call a doctor quick!" Grace Millsap screamed, dabbing at the spreading brown stain with a balled-up napkin. And from somewhere close beside me I thought I heard a soft laugh. But there wasn't anyone there.

Grace Millsap stopped whimpering long enough to glare at me. "You did it! You must have shaken the table — knocked that coffee right into my lap!"

"Oh, come now, Miss Grace, that's impossible. This young lady was nowhere near you." Sam Molloy, who had just come in for a late lunch, ushered her away with a firm arm. "Come on and let's take a look at it now. I believe the worst of it spilled onto your pocketbook . . . here, let me help you. . . ."

I stood staring after them as they shuffled through the front parlor and disappeared down the hall, then jumped as someone touched my arm. Rob Quillian took the coffeepot from me. "Here, let me have that. You look like you could use a break. What happened to old Graceless?"

I sat in the nearest chair. "You wouldn't believe it. Her coffee cup tipped over and burned her. She thinks I did it."

He grinned. "And did you?"

"No, but only because it didn't occur to me. Now, give me back that pot. I have three tables to take care of. I'm fine now, I promise."

He tilted his head and inspected me. "You're sure?"

I stood and made a quick turn. "Positive. See?"

Rob touched my chin with the edge of his hand. "As my grandmama used to say, you look kinda pale and wan to me. Maybe you need some sun."

I thought about that later as Sheri and I cleared the last of the tables and stacked the dishwasher. It was the last Saturday in September, a beautiful day, and I really did need exercise.

"Bailey's always looking for somebody to play tennis," Sheri told me as she scrubbed a pot the second time for Ethelene's inspection. "He and his uncle Kirby used to play all the time. He tried to teach me once, but I kept hitting the ball out of the court." She giggled. "He's so good-looking, it was hard to look at anything but him."

Ethelene took the pan from her and buffed it dry, rubbing it as if it were fine silver. "If you spent half as much time on your chores here as you do mooning over boys, we could cut our work in half. You got plenty of time for that kind of thing, believe me. Don't be in such a hurry!"

Sheri didn't say anything, but she made a face when the housekeeper's back was turned.

84

"Developed too soon," Ethelene told me later when the girl went to spread fresh tablecloths. "All them Griffins do. Why, her great-grandma's the same age as me. Sheri's supposed to be saving to go to some kind of beauty parlor school next year, but it don't look like she'll make it if she can't keep her britches on."

The swinging door from the dining room nudged me from behind as Bailey backed in with an armload of dirty linens. "Sheri said you might be cajoled into a game of tennis," he said. I just looked at him. "Well, maybe she didn't use those exact words," Bailey admitted. "But would you?"

"If you promise not to clobber me, and if Grace Millsap doesn't do me in first. How is she, by the way?"

"Some redness on one thigh, but nothing serious, Sam says. Most of it splashed onto her purse, and the napkin absorbed a lot of it." He grinned. "I hear she accused you of causing the whole thing."

I swept trash into a dustpan and hung the broom on a nail by the door. "I'd have to be a magician. I'm just glad it wasn't worse."

"My God, so am I! I offered to pay any medical expenses and cleaning bills, of course, but I'm afraid we haven't heard the last of it. Did you see it happen? Her hand must have brushed the cup."

"Probably." I threw my apron over the back of a chair. "Just give me a few minutes to change, okay?" Was I the only one who had heard the laughter that came from nowhere?

Contrary to his promise, Bailey was merciless on the tennis court, and after two sets I conceded. All I wanted to do was flop into one of those big old porch rockers and watch the clouds sail by, but in a little more than an hour it would be time to begin serving all over again. I hoped Grace Millsap would eat somewhere else tonight.

"Have you heard anything from that man you were worried about?" Bailey asked as we walked back to the house.

"Gideon? No, and frankly, I haven't had time to think about him. Maybe that's good." Instinctively I glanced at the long upstairs porch, expecting to see my red-haired phantom there, but the swing was where it should be — and it was empty.

Bailey put an arm lightly about me. "Looking for your ghost? Maybe she was the one who dumped the coffee on Grace."

"Maybe she was," I agreed. I don't think he even noticed that I didn't smile at his remark. Dahlia Brown was getting bolder. And apparently I had provoked someone else's interest as well. When I went upstairs to change, I found my sweaters arranged in a tidy stack, and even my socks were folded neatly together. Someone had methodically searched my belongings.

Chapter Eight

I felt as if I had sandbags for feet as I plodded upstairs that night. Good, I thought. I wanted to be so exhausted I would tumble into bed and not hear, see, or move until morning. Not even Mercer Belle's snoring should keep me awake tonight.

It was a warm evening and the cluster of dinner guests — minus Grace Millsap, thank goodness — was in a jovial mood. After they tired of group singing, many stayed to play charades, eventually drifting to the wide front steps. It was almost midnight when Bailey wandered outside, bleary-eyed and grumpy, to tell us to please keep it down, as he was trying to study. He was taking a refresher course in engineering at a branch of the university two mornings a week and had spent most of the evening in his study.

"Why engineering?" I had asked him earlier. I couldn't imagine what use he would have for it at Plumb-Nelly.

He looked at me as if I were ten years old again. "Well, it was my major. I don't want to forget everything. Sometimes I think my brain cells are beginning to stagnate."

I didn't think that likely to happen to someone who read as extensively as Bailey Davenport did, but I kept my mouth shut. He didn't seem in a mood to argue. I suspected that Bailey and his sister sometimes resented the fact that their mother had remarried after their father's death and left them to run the tavern.

From an upstairs window I watched the last taillight disappear down the drive. Eugenia's door was closed, her room dark and silent, as was Delaney's. Mrs. Abernathy's spasmodic sputtering erupted from the small room at the end of the narrow back hallway, and I heard Rob shove open his window and toss his shoes on the floor as I stepped inside my room. Agnes the cat, who had made a nest of the new burgundy sweater I had left on the window seat, abandoned it for my pillow as if we were on the best of terms. I was too sleepy to care.

But for some reason my irrational mind chose that night to be the vigilant caretaker, the ever-wakeful guardian of the inn. Not a sound went undetected: the flushing of a toilet in a room off the front hall; someone (probably Bailey) poking about in the kitchen below me; an inquisitive owl who-whoing from somewhere out back. And then all was quiet. At last I could sleep. If only the swing would stop squeaking.

What fool would be out on the porch making all that racket in the middle of the night? I flopped over on my stomach and smashed the pillow over my head, shoving the cat to the floor, where she glared at me with jack-o'-lantern eyes. The measured creaking continued.

Without turning on a light I fumbled for the worn cotton sweat suit I had crammed into the bottom drawer, pulled on the first two socks I could find, and shoved my feet into sneakers. I knew who was in the swing, knew she was waiting for me. Closing my door softly behind me, I crept down the deserted back passage and into the front hall to the wide double doors. Dahlia Brown set her daisies on the seat beside her and stood to greet me.

The inside of my body felt as if I had inhaled a huge gulp of Arctic air. I couldn't move. The rational part of me resisted, refused to accept her as real. She was a dream, fantasy. But my fanciful self saw the glimmer of mirth in her eyes, smelled her perfume — a light, airy fragrance with a touch of spice. I found myself stepping onto the porch. "What do you want?" I said.

Her eyes took on an urgent expression,

and Dahlia Brown began to move toward the door and me.

I stepped back. I could feel my toes curling under as a scented breeze passed by. And I think I closed my eyes. When I opened them, she was gone.

I stood in the hallway with only a pale moon for light. My hand touched the white wainscoting behind me; it was solid and real. I wasn't dreaming. I whirled about so suddenly it must have made me dizzy, because I had to hold to the jamb for a minute. And then I saw her again — a gauzy cloud of light. I followed her down the wide hall, the twisting stairs, but the only footsteps I heard were my own.

Through the quiet lower corridor we walked like two naughty children playing a forbidden game of follow the leader — past the shadowy parlor, the dining room, the suite where Bailey slept. She stood on the back porch waiting, a graceful, translucent creature in a swirling summer dress. It made me cold to look at her. I shivered, wishing I had worn an extra sweater. But Dahlia Brown was beyond such earthly discomforts and moved into the yard, skirting the pecan grove, flitting past the old pump house. She didn't pause to look back.

A will-o'-the-wisp, she played with me,

disappearing now and again, only to materialize a few yards ahead in a taunting whirl of iridescent fog. I stumbled along the rutted farm road, passed the storage shed where Rob kept his equipment. I thought I had lost her near the old stone smokehouse, then saw her again as she waltzed past a lean-to stacked with firewood.

I stopped for a minute, tucking my hands under my arms for warmth. On my left a sagging gate to an abandoned chicken coop squealed in the wind. Dark silhouettes of cedars, so tall I could scarcely see their tops, marched along the roadside, blocking everything from view. I had no idea where we were going. And then the road curved and I knew. The barn.

It was big and dark and dirty, and it smelled of mice. No, not mice, rats. I stopped at what was left of the door and held to a rusted handle. Was I supposed to go inside?

She waited just ahead of me, an irregular smear of light in this bleak, filthy place. "What is it?" I asked. I felt like a fool talking to somebody who wasn't really there. Or was she? She didn't answer but moved to one side, hesitating just below the loft.

I took one step inside. The old boards groaned. Somewhere in a far black corner something scurried across the floor, and I know I must've yelled. I was shivering so, I don't think a hundred blankets could have warmed me. "Look," I said. "I want to help you, but this place isn't safe. Besides, I can't see a thing. Can't we come back in the day-time?" I wasn't surprised to discover my voice shook too.

She just stood looking at me. Waiting. I could barely see her face, but she looked so desolate standing there, it made me want to cry. All I could think about was the cold; it wasn't just early-autumn cold, but chilling cold. The kind that makes you feel gray in-side. I think I moaned. Somebody did. Dahlia Brown was still there.

"What do you want?" I asked again. No answer. And she wasn't going away. I made some sort of noise and took another step, then another, edging around what appeared to be a broken rocking chair, then yelled when my foot kicked something hard and solid that bumped across the floor.

"Oh, my Lord! What was that?" I looked at her as if I expected an answer, but still she lingered with that same forlorn expres-sion. "I hate this! Hate it!" I said. I shuffled a few inches farther. I didn't know what else to do. Could things get any worse?

They could. I never knew fear could hurt, but I felt as if I had been run through with a butcher knife when I heard the sound of footsteps on the hard-packed earth outside. I gulped cold air and bent double in an effort to hide behind the debris. I should have stayed in bed. I should have stayed in Florida! My heart beat so fast my chest ached. Someone called my name.

"Ginger? Ginger, where in the devil are you?" Rob Quillian let the tilting door slam against the wall. "I know you're in there somewhere."

I stood slowly and moved back toward the door, feeling my way with my feet. "Here," I said. "I'm here." Dahlia Brown was gone.

Rob reached out a warm human hand to help me. "I know there must be a logical reason, but humor me anyway. What are you doing out here at almost three in the morning, sleepwalking?"

He tried to retrieve his arm as we walked outside, but I wouldn't give it up. I didn't object when he put the other one around me. Would I ever be warm again? And to my great embarrassment, I started to cry!

"Hey, it's okay now. Let's get you inside. You're freezing, and no wonder. That barn is like an icehouse." Rob gave my fingers a squeeze as he half carried, half dragged me back to the tavern. We stopped at the kitchen door. "Are you all right now? Ginger, what's going on?"

"I think so. How did you know where I was?" I followed him into the kitchen and sat at the long plank table while he filled the kettle with water. The faucet, I noticed, was still leaking.

"I heard you — or somebody. I didn't know it was you until I saw you tiptoeing downstairs. And then I followed you outside."

"What else did you see?" I asked.

Rob turned on a flame under the kettle. "What was I supposed to see?"

He wasn't going to believe me, but I told him anyway. He didn't laugh hysterically; he didn't even smile. "Dahlia Brown. You saw Dahlia Brown, the girl in the painting?"

I nodded, still shivering. Rob took Ethelene's old brown cardigan that hung by the door and draped it around my shoulders, his hands hesitating on my arms. "Tell me about her," he said.

And I did. "I'm not crazy," I said. "In fact, my grandmother claims I'm the most practical member of the family. Believe it or not, I've never seen a ghost before."

Rob made tea in a bright blue pot and poured it into sturdy mugs. "What do you suppose she wants?" he asked.

I took a sip. It was strong and good.

"I think she wants me to find out how she died."

"But why you? Why now?"

"They're moving her grave, remember? And because I'm her niece, her namesake. My grandmother, Mama Kate, and Dahlia Brown were sisters. Her name was Martha Virginia and she disappeared just before she turned twenty-one. My grandmother never knew what happened to her — until now."

Rob leaned closer to look at me. He hadn't taken the time to comb his straight brown hair, and it stuck out at a peculiar angle over his forehead. His eyes were a comfortable gray. "I should have guessed," he said. "Is that why you're here?"

I warmed my hands with steam from the cup. "Well, partly. I needed to get away for a while." Rob put away a healthy slice of Ethelene's carrot cake as I told him about Gideon Foster. "And you haven't heard from him since?" he asked.

"No, and let's hope I don't." I yawned, declining another cup of tea. "Look, please don't say anything about what happened tonight. I did tell Bailey about my problems with Gideon, but no one else knows I'm related to Dahlia Brown. I'd just as soon they didn't."

Rob stood and kissed my forehead. "They

haven't a ghost of a chance of finding out from me." He made a big production out of rubbing his eyes as he stared at my feet. "Hey, I like that! Are you going to wear the other pair tomorrow?"

I looked down. Even with my bleary eyesight it was impossible to miss my contrasting socks: one bright yellow and the other a vivid purple stripe. "Who knows?" I said. "Maybe I'll start a fad."

We tried to be quiet as we tiptoed through the dark hallway and up the stairs, but I saw a light go out in Bailey's room just before his door closed softly. Again Rob took my hand as we reached the top. "Are you sure you're okay?" he asked.

"I will be if I can just get a few hours' sleep. But tomorrow I'm going to find out what's in that barn that Dahlia wants me to see."

Rob left me at the door to my room. "Not tomorrow," he reminded me. "Today."

Chapter Nine

"Has anybody seen my new sweater?" I said to Sheri's back. I tried to keep my tone light and casual, but I wanted to shove her lacquered little head into a sink full of dirty dishwater.

"What sweater?" She trailed a broom across the kitchen floor and made a big to-do about sweeping under the table. She never cleaned there unless Ethelene was watching.

"The burgundy turtleneck that was airing on the back porch. I know it was there before lunch." I took clean warm plates from the dishwasher and stood on tiptoe to stack them in the cabinet. Somehow between serving an enormous Sunday breakfast and feeding a crowd of hungry churchgoers I had managed to brush the cat hairs from my new purchase and had spread it on a clean towel out of the sun.

Sheri threw the broom in a corner and shrugged. "I don't know. Ask Delaney."

Delaney Davenport probably had three sweaters to each one of mine; besides, except to nod briefly to her over the after-church crowd in the dining room I hadn't seen her all day. I was almost certain that Sheri had "borrowed" my new sweater, but there was no way I could prove it. She had oohed and aahed over it the day I brought it home from the store, hinting that she had a skirt that would go perfectly with it — and it was exactly her size too.

I was glad when she put on her third coat of lipstick and left. Sunday was paper-plate-and-sandwich night for those of us who lived at the tavern, and for another five days I wouldn't have to wait on anybody but myself.

The skies were gray and a chilling drizzle had begun to fall when Rob and I finally escaped from curious eyes and walked to the barn. The old building looked even more forbidding in the gloom of the wet afternoon, and I was glad Rob had thought to bring a flashlight.

The place still smelled of musty hay even though it hadn't been used as a barn for years, and that familiar chill surrounded us as soon as we stepped inside. By the beam of the flashlight I saw the object I had kicked the night before. It was an old rusty can of paint. Obviously someone had meant to spruce up the rocking chair that barred our way.

The dark, damp smell of the afternoon seeped into corners, and a board groaned under my foot. I couldn't see where I was going. What was to keep me from stepping through the floor?

"Where did you say she was standing?" Rob asked, casting the light around.

I pointed. "Over by that wall. Looks like a door back there to a storeroom or something. Do you think she wants us to look inside?"

"Don't ask me; she's your ghost, but we can see." He stepped carefully around a stack of lumber and pulled me along behind him. The old leather handle came off in Rob's hands, but he managed to pry open the door. I stepped aside to give him room. Whatever was inside that room, it (or they) knew we were here now. What if there was a rat in there? A family of rats? I let Rob go in first.

I didn't see a rat, but the dust almost choked me. Since there was no window, we had to depend on the flashlight to see where we were going, but it didn't take long to discover the small room was piled with junk. Rob blew dust from an ancient radio. "An antiques dealer would love to get his hands on some of this stuff. Look at that headboard — looks like cherry."

But I had my eye on something in the

corner and waded through a rusty collection of tricycles and a coat rack made of antlers to reach it. Don't think about mice, I told myself. Or spiders. Or anything that scurries and lives in the dark. I moved aside an early doll carriage with tiny glass windows in its hood, a high chair with a broken tray. "Throw the light this way. I think I've found something!" I called, scrambling to uncover what lay beneath.

Rob held the light over my shoulder. "My God, how did you know?"

"One end of it was sticking up," I said as we wrestled it out together. The old wicker swing was still in one piece. And it was still green.

"Is that what we were supposed to find?" Rob asked as we hurried back to the warm house.

"I don't think so," I said. "We already knew about the swing from the portrait. The artist painted it that way. Besides, I don't see how it could have anything to do with the way Dahlia died. There must be something else. I wish Bailey's aunt Lucy would come home! From what I've heard, she seemed to know Dahlia better than anyone."

"Isn't that Kirby Whitworth's station wagon parked out back?" Rob asked. "Why don't you ask him if he's heard from her?"

We found Bailey's uncle Kirby unloading boxes of produce from the back of the wagon and hurried to give him a hand.

"These darn acorn squash are heavier than I thought," he admitted, hoisting a carton to the porch in one smooth motion. "Had a bumper crop this year — they just won't stop!"

I trailed him to the car for a sackful of sweet potatoes while Rob carried in the remaining bags. "Did you remember to bring those onions?" Rob said. "I told Bailey I'd make my Brunswick stew this week."

"Ten pounds be enough?" Kirby asked, swinging a lumpy sack to his shoulder.

"Probably not, but I'll get more from The Store. It's my grandmama's recipe," Rob explained. "She put onions in everything but ice cream."

"We've been poking around out in the barn," I told Kirby as we went inside together, "and you'll never guess what we found!"

He washed his hands at the sink. "A lot of junk, I'll bet. The Davenports never throw anything away."

I told him about the swing. "It used to hang on the upstairs porch," I said. "It's the same one that's in the painting. I thought your wife might tell us about the girl in the swing.

Wasn't she a friend of hers?"

He nodded. "Lucy was most upset over that girl's death. She felt partially responsible, you know; the woman was living here — working at Plumb-Nelly."

"Do you remember her?" I asked.

"Oh, yes! A beautiful girl — an actress. Always laughing about something, it seemed, and didn't hesitate to speak her mind. It shocked everyone when she died." Kirby Whitworth filled a glass with water and drank it without stopping. "Wonder if Ethelene left any of those oatmeal cookies from yesterday?"

I offered him the jar. "When do you expect your wife back from Europe?"

"Next week probably. Woodrow should be through with his campaigning around here by then, and Lucy avoids that like she does the kitchen!" He laughed as he wiped crumbs across his broad chest. "Our son's running for lieutenant governor," he said, planting a printed card in my hand. "Don't forget him on election day, now."

I didn't have the heart to tell him I couldn't vote in North Carolina.

Kirby Whitworth took two more cookies from the jar and wrapped them in a paper napkin as if they were fine jewels. "If you want to know about the girl in that painting," he told us, "you might talk to Chamblee Davenport. He painted that picture, you know. We all thought he was in love with her."

But my employer didn't seem to want to discuss the subject when I mentioned it at work the next day. In fact, he pretended not to hear me at all. "He's funny about that old picture," Anne Hughes, the receptionist, told me later. "I asked him about it once, told him he ought to do more like it." She frowned. "I think he got kind of irritated with me — said that was the last one he intended to do and he wished he hadn't even painted that! He just does pictures of old barns now, tumbledown houses — things like that."

But I wasn't through with Chamblee Davenport. He was the closest link I had to Dahlia Brown, and I was determined to discover what he knew about her life — and possibly her death — in Fiddler's Glen.

"What is it worth to you to find out?" Rob asked after dinner that night when I told him about my difficulties.

"What do you mean?"

He skimmed through a stack of music and rolled his eyes at me. "Eugenia has three for bridge — including your friend Chamblee," he said. "She's looking for a fourth."

"No way!" I plucked a sheet of music from

the pile. "Here, let's do this."

He laughed. "Are you sure? That's an instrumental — 'The Flight of the Bumblebee.' " Rob reared back and began to play "Swing Low, Sweet Chariot" without any music at all. "Oh, go on!" he told me. "I'm in the mood to improvise tonight. You might learn something; besides, Eugenia's really a sweetie."

I wasn't so sure about that. I looked at her tapping the deck of cards with her long red nails. And then she saw me and the trap was set. "Virginia!" she bellowed with her slash of a smile, then patted the chair next to her. "Hurry up, we've been waiting for you!"

An hour later I still didn't know what I was doing, but my partner, Mercer Belle Abernathy, didn't seem to care. So far she had munched her way through a large bowl of popcorn, about half a jar of taffy, and a mug of cider. As long as we didn't run out of food, maybe I could survive the night.

Eugenia looked at me with pity as I attempted to play a hand, and poured herself another cup of the strange pink tea I later learned was sassafras. "Lead out your trumps, Virginia, but make sure you have an entrance to the board," she said. I nodded numbly and glanced at Chamblee Davenport, who was keeping our one-sided score. So far I hadn't had the courage to bring Dahlia Brown into the conversation. I would have to work it in somehow.

But Eugenia saved me the trouble. "What in the world were you and Rob doing out in that old barn yesterday in all that rain? It must leak like a sieve, and I'll bet it's full of rats."

"That's not all it's full of," I said. "We found that old swing out there — the one that's in the painting."

Bailey's uncle Chamblee took the trick and led off with my ace of trumps. He didn't say a word.

"Bailey says they're moving her grave," I said.

Mercer Belle crumpled a candy wrapper and looked at me over her cards. "I'm glad she's finally going home. I heard her, you know — swinging out there on that empty porch. Heard her feet hit the floor and kinda drag — like they do when you're in a swing."

Across the room Rob played old tunes from a yellowed booklet, apparently oblivious to us. He smiled to himself. *Let's have another cup of coffee . . . let's have another piece of pie . . .*

I hoped it wouldn't give Mercer Belle ideas. "Wonder what took them so long to locate her family," she said.

"I guess they assumed she didn't have any," Eugenia told her.

Chamblee Davenport scooped up the last trick, setting us again. "I knew she had family," he announced to no one in particular. "A sister. She wrote her every week."

"Maybe she never mailed the letters," I said.

He shook his head. "She mailed them. Sent them out faithfully, but nobody ever answered. I watched her wait by that mailbox day after day, and that sister — or whoever she wrote to — didn't even care enough to write once!"

"Then why didn't you write her? Let her know when the girl died?" Eugenia asked.

"Don't you think I tried? We couldn't find an address. Anything. Sometimes I think we imagined her."

I glanced at Rob to see if he was absorbing this, but he was sliding into another song, one I'd heard my grandmother sing. The words made me think of a picture post card. They told of a winding path that led to a cottage by the sea where someone with blue eyes waited — ever smiling, of course. It was a soppy, sentimental song. Naturally it made me want to cry.

Chamblee pushed back his chair and stared

at Rob, but he didn't get up. "Why are you playing that?"

Rob glanced up sharply at the edge in his voice. "It's in the book. Why?"

The older man held out his hand. "Could I see it please?"

"Of course." Rob crossed the room and gave it to him.

Chamblee Davenport flipped through the pages. "Where did you find this?"

"Why, it was in the piano bench," Rob said. "Is something wrong?"

"I suppose not, but it seems so strange . . ." Chamblee carefully opened the book to the inside cover. "It was hers, you see. There's her name. I gave it to her myself." He placed the old book on the table and smoothed the frayed cover. For him, I thought, the rest of us weren't even here. "That song you were playing," he said. "It was her favorite. She sang it for me the night she died."

"Chamblee Davenport has blue eyes," I told Rob after everyone had gone to bed.

He gave me a puzzled look. "That's nice, Ginger."

"Like the person in the song," I said. "Remember? Do you think they were in love?"

"Looks that way." Rob gently placed the song book on the piano. We had offered it to Chamblee, but he wouldn't accept it. "It belongs here," he said. "Besides, I don't even have a piano."

"But that's not what really bothers me," Rob said. "That book wasn't in the bench the other night. Remember? We went through every bit of that music. I want to know who put it there!"

I just smiled at him. "Don't you know?" I said.

Chapter Ten

Rob and I turned out the lights in the parlor and were getting ready to go upstairs, when the front door closed with an angry, unyielding sound and someone stumbled into the hall. I started to see who it was, but Rob put a hand out to stop me, and when I heard Bailey speak, I was glad he had.

"For God's sake, go on up to bed! You don't need another drink."

Delaney giggled and I heard a piece of furniture totter — probably the ladderback chair that stood by the desk. "Oh, don't be such a drudge, Bailey, I'm fine! Why did you have to come and spoil all the fun? I could've made it home okay by myself."

"Don't delude yourself! If Charlie McDowell hadn't called me, we would've had to scrape you off of that big tree down at the curve. You're in no shape to drive — or do anything else, for that matter. And who was that man you were with? It sure as hell wasn't Sam Molloy!"

The expression in Rob's eyes was almost comical. What could we do? I wished there

110

were some way to let them know we were there. But it was too late now.

The chair skidded again. Delaney probably had kicked it. "Sam Molloy's on call at the hospital tonight. And last night his son's scout troop had a parents' meeting! If you like the good doctor so much, *you* wait around for him!" Delaney's voice grew louder. "I'm bored. I've worked hard all week, and I'm tired of doing nothing."

"Shut up! Do you want to wake everybody in the house? If you want to go out with lounge lizards, fine, but it isn't smart to pick up strangers in bars, Delaney. That character you were with looked pretty slimy to me. Thank God the bartender knew who you were!" Bailey's tone softened. "Come on, we'll go out to the kitchen. You need something in your stomach."

I looked at Rob. If they came through the parlor they would surely see us for the eavesdroppers we were. But Delaney wasn't interested in food just then. "Uh — I don't feel so good, Bailey . . . I think I'm gonna be sick!"

I heard him scuttle her into the bathroom under the stairs, where somebody turned on the water full force — thank goodness. Rob and I just about knocked each other down racing upstairs.

111

"Well, that explains why I haven't seen Sam Molloy for the last couple of days," Rob whispered when we reached the back corridor. "I guess the poor guy's been given his papers."

"Looks that way," I agreed. Frankly, I thought the young doctor was lucky, but for once I kept my mouth shut.

The next morning I found Bailey waiting for me in the parlor. "I want to apologize for the disturbance we made in the hallway last night," he said. "I had no idea you and Rob were in here."

"What?" I'm sure I looked confused. I hadn't had my coffee yet.

"I saw you on the stairs." He frowned. "Guess we woke everybody within a five-mile radius. Sorry."

"Don't worry about it. I'm sorry too." What else could I say? "Is Delaney all right?"

He laughed. "I hope not! I'm afraid my sister's having a little trouble growing up."

We both looked up at the sound of Eugenia's cane in the upstairs hall, and Bailey took my hand for a few seconds. "I haven't had a chance to tell you, but we all appreciate your stepping in and helping us out. I'm glad you decided to stay." He pressed my hand before letting it go, and we escaped in different directions before prying Mrs. T.S.S. came upon us.

I couldn't deny that I was attracted to Bailey Davenport, and I could still feel the touch of his hand as I sat over my corn flakes and bananas. There were times when I thought there might be something between us; and then he would be professionally polite, almost distant, or absent himself entirely as he had for the past few days. Until this morning. And I smiled so brightly at Rob as he came into the dining room that he almost walked into Sheri with a tray of pancakes.

He sat across from me. "You look like you got a full night's sleep. No spectral company?"

"No, but I expected it. I could almost feel her there in the room with us when you were playing that song. She's getting impatient, Rob." I looked at him as he toyed with a pink chrysanthemum in the bud vase. "You don't believe all this, do you?"

"You ask a lot, Ginger Cameron, but I'm trying. Really."

It was hard to stay upset with somebody with a smile as nice as Rob's; besides, I couldn't blame him. He ate half of my banana and helped himself to a doughnut. He had already had his breakfast and wasn't hungry, he assured me. "Okay, tell me," he said without a trace of his usual levity, "we know there was something going on between your aunt and Chamblee Davenport. And there's a link with the barn too. What do you think it could be?"

I drank my juice before he got thirsty. "Well, aside from the fact that they had their plays there, it could have been the setting for something else — something to do with her death."

"You think she was killed there? Didn't they find her body below a cliff somewhere?"

"That doesn't mean anything," I told him. "It could've been thrown there. Why would anybody have a reason to question a fall?" I lowered my voice as Sheri walked by. "There's something in that barn she wants us to find." I almost told him about my experience in the cemetery with the Masonic emblems, but I had trouble believing it myself.

"There's a trouble light around here somewhere," Rob said as we left the dining room. "I'll try to find a long extension cord, and we'll see what we come up with out there."

"There's something else I mean to find out," I said, "but I'll have to take a day off to do it."

He hesitated at the door. "What's that?"

"I want to know why Mama Kate never got those letters."

When I got home from work that night I found my new burgundy sweater folded neatly in my drawer. It smelled of cheap perfume and had a blob of something like pizza sauce on the front. I marched downstairs and shoved Sheri Griffin into the laundry room.

"Hey! What's the matter with you? Leave me alone! I've got customers out there." I must have looked fierce. The girl was terrified. Good.

I held the sweater in front of her. "I am having this cleaned," I said. "And when I get the bill, I'm giving it to you! I don't mind letting you borrow things as long as you have the courtesy to ask, and provided you take care of them, but I would like a chance to wear them first."

She tried to slide past me. "You're crazy. I don't know what you're talking about."

"Then maybe your mother would know. I'm sure she saw you before you left on your date last night — or wherever it was you went. I'll bet you told her I let you wear it, didn't you, Sheri?"

She grabbed my arm in a viselike grip. "Oh, Lord, don't! Please don't . . . she doesn't even know I went out!" Tears spilled over and started to smear her mascara.

"What on earth made you do a thing like that? All you had to do was ask!"

"I was afraid you'd say no." Sheri snuffled. "You won't say anything to Ethelene, will you?"

I tore off a paper towel and wet it at the laundry sink. "This is just between the two of us. Here, you look like a raccoon. I don't know why you wear all that stuff anyway. You're pretty enough without it."

"Thanks, you really think so?" Sheri wiped the smudges from beneath her eyes. "That better?"

I nodded. "And you're right, I would've said no — at least until I'd worn it awhile myself." Sheri sniffed. Her lip trembled. Good grief, was she going to start crying again? "Hey, look," I said. "I do have some other things you might want to look at. Why don't you come by my room when you have a few minutes and we'll go through my closet?"

"Really? That would be great!" Sheri splashed water on her puffy face. "And Ginger, I'm sorry about the sweater."

"You're going to be even sorrier when you get the cleaning bill," I said. I smiled when I said it, but I meant every word.

Bailey was greeting guests in the front hallway as I started to my room, but he called to me before I reached the top of the stairs. "How would you like to get away from here for a while?" he asked. "I'm in the mood for Italian food."

I thought about the pizza sauce on my sweater. "How about Chinese?" I said.

We settled for steak and fries, then took in a play, a local production of *Harvey*. I didn't have a bit of trouble identifying with Elwood P. Dowd. Seeing creatures who weren't there was becoming a way of life at Plumb-Nelly Tavern.

I must have been smiling about that during the drive home, as I found Bailey looking at me when we stopped for a light. "Keeping in mind the rate of inflation . . . a quarter for your thoughts?" he said.

"Just thinking about the play," I said. Should I tell him about our ghost in residence? I wasn't sure it was time. Besides, his grandparents would have been a young couple living at Plumb-Nelly then. How did I know they hadn't been involved in my aunt's death?

"I hope you won't think Delaney's lost it completely," he said after driving silently for a while. "She's spoiled, I know, but it's more than that. I think she misses our father. He and Delaney were always close. Her own marriage didn't work out, and then Mother remarried and moved to Maine. . . ." Bailey pulled into his usual parking place under the sycamore tree and sighed. "I suppose she must feel deserted."

"What about you?" I asked as we walked the narrow flagstone path to the porch.

He looked down at me with the beginning of a smile. "Me? Well, not at the moment." He pulled me close as we stood by the lilac bush near the front steps, and I wondered how many couples had kissed in this spot.

Unfortunately we were not to be one of them — at least not then. Just as his lips were about to meet mine in what I hoped would be an ardent (and I could accept passionate) kiss, something crashed on the walk a few feet away and shattered with a noise loud enough to wake the dead. Only the dead — or one of them — was already awake. And this time she was waiting in my room.

I should have guessed, because Agnes wouldn't even follow me into the back corridor, and the room had that peculiar pressed-flower smell. At first I sensed rather than saw her, and then she began to take form: a wispy, willowy shadow with definite feminine curves. I didn't even bother to turn on the light. "I don't suppose you ever sleep?" I said.

She gathered herself by the window, and even in the darkness I could see the summer-morning green of her eyes. Tucking my feet under me, I sat on the bed. My words sounded filtered, as if they had seeped through cotton. "Look, I want to help you," I told her, "but we have to get one thing straight: You're going to have to stay out of my love life. That little trick with the flowerpot out there takes the trophy for bad timing, so stop it!"

I think I scared myself. And the mist that was Dahlia Brown began to dissolve. Maybe I had gone too far? But she had only moved closer; the cool air around her smelled like a cedar chest. Her dress was of shifting rainbow colors: green, pink, yellow, blending into themselves and gathered with a wide band of lavender around her waist.

I sat up straighter. Where should I begin? "This has something to do with the barn, doesn't it?"

Her eyes seemed to grow brighter.

"But it's not in the storage room?" I stopped for a minute and listened. What if someone heard me in here talking? Playing charades with a ghost? Dahlia Brown looked at me sadly; time was running out, and I was probably her last chance. "Then

I guess you're going to have to show me," I told her.

I grabbed the long green cape I had had since college, which was the first thing I could find without turning on a light, and started after her down the narrow hallway. I thought once of waking Rob, but I was afraid he might frighten Dahlia away. On second thought, I wondered, how do you frighten a ghost? No light showed from beneath his closed door, and I didn't want to chance waking the sonorous Mercer Belle by knocking. And this time I remembered to take the flashlight I knew Rob kept in the cloakroom downstairs.

I felt a little like Brontë's Catherine pursuing her fierce Heathcliff across the moors as I slogged to the barn in my green cape and hood, but it was blanket-warm and cozy, and I was glad of it — especially when I stepped inside. It wasn't just cold. It was frigid.

My fingers closed around the splintery handle of a rake left leaning inside the doorway, and I took a step forward. A little stick of wood wasn't going to protect me from a ghost — but I knew somehow it wasn't the ghost who might harm me.

Dahlia Brown waited in the same place a few feet from the far right wall. Only the vague outlines of objects were visible in the dark loft above her, and I thought I heard a faint creaking in the rafters. Could someone be hiding there? "Who's there?" I croaked. I had trouble breathing. What if somebody *answered?*

"Could we please get this over with?" I asked. "I'm not crazy about this place!" I threw the beam of light above her to reveal a couple of large picture frames and a rolled-up carpet. Or it looked like a rolled-up carpet. "Is it up there?" I asked. I hoped not. There was no way I was going to explore that loft at night!

Still, Dahlia didn't move. She seemed to be looking for something on the floor where she stood. I cast the light about her, but all I could see was fifty years of clutter and debris. "Where?" I said. If I had reached out I could have touched her — if there had been anything there to touch. "I don't see anything here."

When I looked up she was fading — from the feet up, a little at a time. And the last thing I saw was her sad, sad eyes until they disappeared as well.

Chapter Eleven

There was something about the back porch that made me stop at the edge of the clearing: a shadow that didn't belong there. And then the shadow became two and I heard a woman's low laughter. Had Delaney changed her mind about Sam Molloy? The silhouettes merged again and I drew my cloak about me and watched jealously, having been cheated out of my own moment of passion a short time before.

A stiff wind came up, but the lovers didn't seem to notice. I took refuge under a pecan tree and hugged myself for warmth. Would they never leave? I was getting a severe cramp in my leg when the two finally parted company. The man walked around the side of the house to a car that must have been parked out front, and Delaney went inside through the kitchen. I gave her a few minutes and followed.

Bailey Davenport stood in the hall at the foot of the stairs. I took one step back into the shadows, but he had already seen me. "Ginger? Was that you I heard a few minutes ago?" He seemed to be looking around; I suppose he thought I wasn't alone.

I shrugged out of my cape and let it slip over my arm. If he had stood very still and listened, he would have heard his sister's door close softly overhead. "Thought I'd left some aspirin in my car," I said. "I had one whopper of a headache." That wasn't so very far from the truth. I could feel one sneaking up on me. I frowned convincingly — or so I thought.

He moved to the old cherry desk that stood behind him and pulled open a bottom drawer, setting a large bottle of tablets before me. "Help yourself," he said, then disappeared into his room. I don't think he believed me for a minute.

"Where in the world are you two going with all that?" Eugenia asked. I had left work a little early the next day while there was still plenty of daylight, and now hurried down the old pasture road to catch up with Rob, who had what looked like about a mile of orange extension cord looped around his arm. He turned and grinned at Eugenia, who trailed after us. "I'm going to lower Ginger down the old well and see how long it takes before she makes a splash," he said. "Want to come along and watch?"

Eugenia walked a little faster. She had forgotten to bring her cane. "She's too skinny to make a splash! You think it will take long? I don't want to be late for dinner."

I laughed. "We're going to the barn," I explained. "I lost an earring out there."

"I've never noticed you wearing earrings," she said, giving me a closer look. "What's it look like?"

I did wear earrings occasionally, but recently I hadn't taken the trouble. I did a mental inventory of my jewelry box. "Gold studs," I said. "Tiny gold studs. They're so small you probably wouldn't notice them."

"Then why wear them?" Eugenia said as she stalked back to the house.

"That was close," I told Rob as we unwound the cord from the toolshed, which had an electrical outlet, to the barn on the other side of the road. "I thought she'd follow us all the way."

"It wouldn't matter if she did," he said. "Unless your friendly ghost makes an appearance. Think she will?"

"I doubt it. She gave me a pretty good idea where to look last night."

Rob snaked a vivid orange trail over a ditch and through the gate to the barnyard. "Not much gets past our Eugenia. I'm surprised she hasn't met your late aunt herself." He paused to pull open the door. "Think she bought that story about the earring?"

"No, but it will give me a chance to think of a better one."

"Don't count on it," he said.

Rob held the light while I cleared the area where Dahlia had stood, until nothing was left but dust; the problem was, the dust was at least an inch thick. "I'm going to see if I can find a broom," I said. "I'm sure I saw one out in the toolshed." When I came back I found him examining the cracks in the floor. "There's a lot of stuff down here," he said. "Be careful how you sweep."

It took us over an hour to find it, but when Rob dislodged a gray-looking bead and held it up to the light, I knew our search was over. "It came from the coral necklace," I said. "The one she was wearing in the painting."

With a tug of his long arm he pulled me to my feet. "But was she wearing it when she died?"

Kirby Whitworth said he couldn't remember when I asked him that night at dinner, but did I know if there was any more of that sweet potato pie. I swiped another slice from the kitchen and topped it with a golden square of watermelon rind preserves. He ate it before I could finish my coffee, crossed his hands over his stomach, and smiled. "Now, *that's* good eating! I wonder if I got Lucy the recipe . . . no, it wouldn't do any good."

After a few minutes he frowned at me. "Why the interest in Dahlia Brown? All this happened a long time ago — probably before your parents were born."

I shrugged. "I guess it's because of the painting; she fascinates me in a way. And she's wearing some sort of necklace; I wondered what happened to it, that's all."

He stood with a groan and pushed back his chair. "Well, wish I could help you, but I've never paid much attention to things like that. Lucy says I'm color blind."

I looked at his purple plaid shirt and red sweater and agreed.

Chamblee Davenport scowled at me across his cluttered desk at *The Bugle* the next day. "Why in the world do you want to know that?" he asked.

"I noticed it in the painting," I said. "And it just seemed strange that she would go wandering around by herself at night wearing jewelry as delicate as that."

He burrowed in a deep drawer for a pencil although he had about ten of them on his desk. "Maybe she didn't."

"Well then, where is it? Wouldn't someone have put the necklace away? Saved it?

Unless, of course, she was buried in it."

He kicked the drawer shut. "What does it matter now? Has Ethelene been telling her ghost tales again?"

I didn't answer. That was as good an excuse as any.

Chamblee Davenport laced a pencil through his fingers. "The last time I saw Dahlia she was wearing that same dress she had on in the painting. She always wore the necklace with that." He looked up to meet my eyes. "I don't know what she was wearing when she died."

"Where was she when you last saw her?"

"Why, it was in the barn. It was the final show of the season, and the cast had a party to celebrate." The pencil rolled from his fingers. "It was the same night my sister announced her engagement to Kirby Whitworth."

I frowned. "I wonder who saw her last."

To my surprise, he smiled at me. "I do believe you're trying to dredge up a fifty-year-old mystery, Virginia! Only, for the life of me, I can't imagine why. I think you'd better talk with my sister — as soon as she thinks it's time to come home. She and Dahlia shared a room, you know, for the last few weeks she was here. If anyone can tell you about the necklace, Lucy would be the one."

I took advantage of his mellow mood — and the fact that I'd brought in several substantial accounts — to ask for a day off. "There are some things I need to take care of at home," I explained. "After all, I didn't expect to be here this long when I came."

"Fine, just leave a number where we can reach you," he said. "In case any questions arise."

"I'm not sure where I'll be staying," I told him. "But I'll call."

I had phoned my grandmother earlier to tell her I was coming, and stopped by the tavern that evening only long enough to let Ethelene know when to expect me back. Naturally she insisted on feeding me. "Here, take one of these meat pastries with you," she said. "You can eat it along the way. I'll put in a couple of pears too; and finish those cookies while you're at it." And before I could protest she had packed enough food for three.

Rob pulled wilted marigolds around the birdbath out front. "Going on a picnic?" he asked, leaning back on his long haunches.

I threw my overnight bag in the trunk and set my supper carefully on the seat beside me. Since he knew about my relationship with Dahlia Brown, I didn't see any harm in telling him where I was going. "I have to find out about those letters," I said. "There must be a reason my grandmother never got them." Maybe I would even discover the Masonic connection.

He sauntered over and stood in the shade of a red bud tree. Although it was almost six, the October sun was still warm. "Isn't it a little late for that?" Rob asked.

"Probably, but I have to try." I blew him a kiss. "See you tomorrow."

He gave me his "lost little boy" look. "But who's going to help me entertain tonight?"

"Improvise," I said.

"What letters?" Mama Kate asked the next morning as we cleared away the breakfast dishes. "I never got any letters from Martha."

I almost smiled. I had to remind myself who Martha was; she would always be Dahlia to me.

"What makes you think there were letters?" She paused to glance out the window at my grandfather, who had stopped to chat with the neighbor next door. He was gradually regaining his strength and his daily regimen included a walk around the block.

I told her about Chamblee Davenport and the painting, but I didn't tell her about my nocturnal visits to the barn or what we had found there.

Mama Kate offered me the last piece of cinnamon toast, then absently bit into it before I had time to consider. "Who's Chamblee Davenport?" she asked.

"A very nice man — you'd like him. He's part owner of the weekly where I work, *The Bugle*. I think he was in love with Dah—Martha. Anyway, he said he saw her mail those letters. She wrote every week, he said."

"Then I should've received them . . . unless —" My grandmother whirled about so quickly, she knocked over a box of cereal, scattering oat flakes across the table. And when I saw her face — well, if she hadn't been my grandmother, I would've run for my life! "The aunts," she said. I've never heard so much anger in two syllables.

"Well, I suppose I shouldn't be surprised," Mama Kate said after a long silence. "They intercepted those letters, probably had them held at the post office, and stupid me — I never even suspected!"

I nodded. I had come to the same conclusion. "Do you think they're still here?"

"Aunt Mabel was such a pack rat, I wouldn't be surprised. But I've thrown out a lot of their junk — old letters, things like that." She frowned. "Unless they kept

130

them separate from the rest, hid them some-where. It wouldn't do for me to find them, you know."

I knew. If Mama Kate knew what her aunts had done, the devil would have had to take a backseat.

"Okay, where do we start?" I asked later as we huddled in the cold attic. Downstairs in the sitting room my grandfather and a friend played checkers by a warm fire, and I couldn't help but envy them just a little.

Mama Kate rubbed her hands together for warmth. She looked fragile and tired in the anemic attic light. "We could start with that old oak desk, I guess. Ugly old thing. They kept their accounts in there." She poked about in the pigeonholes. "There are some photographs in here, but I don't remember any letters."

My grandparents had come back to the roomy old Victorian house after the two aunts died, since they had left it to my grand-mother in their will. I had never known them to live anywhere else. I dug into the contents of a cardboard box. "Maybe there's a trunk with a false bottom," I said.

Mama Kate made a face. "You've been reading too many mysteries . . . and leave those things alone!"

I grinned. "Why? What's in here?"

"Just some poetry I wrote in college," she mumbled, turning away.

"You wrote this much poetry?" I flipped through a composition book. "Well, well, well!"

"Forget it!" my grandmother said. "See what's in that chest of drawers over there."

And so I did. I found a purse with a broken clasp, a handknitted muffler (olive drab), and a supply of worn sheets mended many times. The whole thing smelled of moth balls. "If you'd give all this stuff to charity," I said, "they'd probably send you a bill."

"It's past noon," Mama Kate reminded me an hour or so later. "I don't know about you, but my feet are getting numb. Come on and I'll fix us something hot for lunch. Your granddaddy must be starving."

I shoved aside a carton of bad paintings. "These are almost awful enough to win a prize at the art show," I said, stretching to ease the ache in my back. "Have you looked in that old wardrobe?"

She dusted off her hands. "Nothing in there but books."

"What kind of books?"

"Nothing anybody would want. I keep meaning to get rid of them."

I pulled open the mirrored door. "I see what you mean," I said. *"Moral Lessons for*

Today's Child — how boring! Who read this?"

"Why Aunt Eleanor, of course. Aunt Mabel too. They tried to read them to us, but we wouldn't have any part of it," my grandmother said.

I think we just stood and looked at each other for a minute as realization sank in, then Mama Kate gave a funny little yell and took the book from my hands.

We found her sister's letters scattered among the pages.

Chapter Twelve

My grandmother cried as we read the letters together. "Why, they haven't been opened!" she repeated, shaking her head. "Not even the first one. I never believed anyone could be so steel-hearted — even the aunts!"

While my grandfather napped, the two of us sat at the small sewing table by the sitting room window, the letters spread in front of us. The paper was brittle and yellowed and had an acrid, musty smell. The words, written so many years ago, were every bit as dead as Dahlia Brown herself.

The first of them were written in January after my aunt left home and were mailed from Raleigh, where she had joined a newly formed theater troupe. After a few months, Dahlia received an offer to perform with a group called Show Time South and moved on to do summer stock at several resorts, culminating with a two-month run at Plumb-Nelly.

"She was so excited about that," Mama Kate said, passing a tissue-thin sheet to me. "Seems the tavern barn was sort of a plum among actors, and she felt lucky to be a part of it." She pointed out a sentence underlined many times: *Fiddler's Glen, here I come!*

I folded the letter and replaced it carefully in its envelope. If only she had known, I thought. But known what? "Why didn't she call?" I asked. "Surely she must have suspected you weren't getting her letters."

My grandmother looked at me. "Call where? The aunts didn't even get a phone until almost ten years later."

I tried to picture the old barn as it must have been by the way my aunt described it: filled with color and music and applause. And then I saw the name. It stood out like a snowsuit on a beach full of bikinis: *Mason.*

So this was what it was all about! "I wonder who Mason was," I said after reading a brief note written soon after my aunt arrived at the tavern.

Mama Kate looked up. "I don't know, why?"

"She must have known him earlier. She just says, *There's someone here I knew before — I think I wrote you about it. I never expected to find Mason here. Why Fiddler's Glen? I can't imagine!*"

"Maybe he was a member of the troupe — someone she'd met in Raleigh; I don't think she mentioned him though." My grandmother read silently, then reached for my hand. "Ginger, listen, she suspected the aunts' doings. *I know you would write if you were getting my letters, but I'm going to keep sending them anyway — just in case. Please don't give up hoping, Rose, and when this summer's over I'll find a way to reach you, I promise!*" My grandmother smiled. "I knew she wouldn't desert me."

I turned away, then stood to lower the shade against the afternoon sun. I wished I could tell Mama Kate how right she was.

"That's strange," she said a few minutes later. "Here she mentions that fellow again. Look at this: *I just don't know what to do about Mason. This foolishness has got to stop!*"

"What foolishness, I wonder. Does she say anything else about him?"

Mama Kate read the letter again. "No, and this is the last time she wrote."

Mason. This was what my aunt was trying to tell me when she led me to the stones. But Mason *who?* I worried about it during the monotonous drive back to Fiddler's Glen that afternoon. Could Mason have been his last name? I looked for Rob as I turned in at the now-familiar stone columns, hoping he would be working outside. Wouldn't he be surprised to hear about the letters? I couldn't wait to share my news! But it was already getting dark, and even the porch was deserted. I glanced at the gallery above, but it, too, was empty and still.

As soon as I stepped inside I knew why the place had seemed so quiet. Everyone was in the parlor, and they all were trying to talk at once. A tall, lively woman with hair so white it almost hurt my eyes seemed to be the center of all this attention. I say lively because even though she sat sedately in a huge Victorian chair her hands moved constantly as she talked.

She reached out when she saw me, and I had no choice but to go over and take her hands. "You have to be Virginia," she said. "I've heard all about you . . . and my goodness, you're right," she said to Kirby Whitworth, who stood beside her. "She does look very much like Dahlia."

So this was Lucy Whitworth! How could one person create so much activity? The sound of her voice made me smile, and I had a feeling that we would have been close friends if we had the chance. "Bailey says you sing beautifully," she said. "None of us Davenports can carry a tune, you know, but we do like to listen. I hope you're going to sing tonight."

"She'd better. She promised me she would." Rob scooped up a handful of popcorn from the bowl on the table. "What would you like to hear?"

"Something slow and sentimental, I think. I'm in a mellow mood." Lucy Whitworth thumbed through a stack of what looked like quilting scraps in her lap, sorting the bright colors as she spoke.

"What about that music you were playing the other night?" Eugenia said. "From that old book you found." Her bold voice sounded harsh compared to the other woman's rhythmic speech.

"I see you've met Aunt Lucy." Bailey stood behind me, his hands on my shoulders. "Maybe she can tell you about your ghost."

"Do we have to go through all that again?" I said, turning very carefully so I wouldn't dislodge his hands. I liked them very well where they were.

"What ghost?" Lucy Whitworth asked, frowning as she threaded a needle.

"I saw someone who looked like the girl in the painting when I stayed here as a child," I explained. "Just because she had red hair doesn't mean she was a ghost."

Delaney laughed as she played with the cat in front of the fire. "But you saw her swinging on the upstairs porch! There's never been a swing on that north end."

Her aunt didn't laugh. "That's what you

think," she said. "That's where Chamblee painted her portrait — in that old green wicker swing." She knotted her thread and looked at me. "You must have seen that painting somewhere."

"Maybe I did," I said finally. The weight of Bailey's hands on my shoulders suddenly seemed too warm and heavy, and I moved away from the group, catching Rob's eye as I crossed the room.

The corners of his mouth turned up in a smile so momentary, I wondered if I'd imagined it. "I understand you two were roommates," he said to Lucy.

She wove her needle in a row of dainty stitches. "And friends," she said solemnly.

Sheri came to the door just then to announce that dinner was served, and Bailey ushered me in along with his aunt. As she was being seated, she put her hand on my arm. "Sometime we'll talk about Dahlia," she whispered. "That is, if you'd like to."

"I would like to," I said. "I'd like to very much." But how did she know?

I was glad Chamblee Davenport wasn't there for the musical entertainment that night, because we ended up having a sing-along out of Dahlia's old songbook, and I discovered Lucy wasn't lying about not being able to carry a tune. As we stood together by the piano during a lull in the evening, I was tempted to ask her about the coral beads, but there were too many people around. And I wasn't sure how to explain my curiosity.

Delaney took off mysteriously after supper without a word to anyone, and the Whitworths excused themselves early. Mercer Belle fell asleep by the fire, and when she couldn't get a bridge game going, Eugenia swept upstairs to bed with annoyed thumps of her cane.

After the last dinner guest left, Rob yawned as he closed the piano. "I think I'll walk off some of Ethelene's cottage pudding," he said, lingering in the doorway. It was an open invitation for me to follow, but sometimes I'm slow to react. The two of us hadn't had a chance to talk alone since I returned from Mama Kate's, and I was about to tell him to wait, when Bailey quietly took my hand. I stayed.

The old tavern grew dark and quiet around us, and the fire died to a few red coals while we sat holding hands in the parlor, just as my aunt and Chamblee Davenport had probably done years before. Bailey told me about the class he was taking and of his worries over Delaney. "I know she's seeing somebody," he said. "God only knows who it is! My sister's never been a very good judge of character, especially when it comes to men."

I didn't tell him about seeing Delaney and her latest love interest saying good night behind the tavern, although I knew he didn't believe my story about the aspirin. Delaney Davenport was a grown woman. If she wanted to drag home the dregs, that was her business, not mine — or Bailey's.

My head rested on his shoulder as we heard Delaney's car in the drive, and a few minutes later the stairs creaked as she went up to her room. Neither of us moved. Bailey stroked my arm, holding me closer. "Ginger, you aren't . . . well, maybe you are . . . *are* you seeing anyone special?" he asked an inch or so from my ear. It tickled.

In the dim light I saw the outline of his face and touched his chin with my finger. "What do you mean by *seeing?*" I knew, of course, but when did he think I would have time to date somebody?

"Oh, hell! I guess I'm asking if you're interested in anybody. Back home — at your grandmother's, I mean."

I started to laugh. "You thought I was going home for some kind of wild, romantic rendezvous!" (If he only knew!) "Do you want a note from my grandmother?"

"Ginger, look — I'm sorry. I didn't mean it the way it sounded. It's just that — well, you may have guessed — I look at you in a different way since the days when you wore chocolate on your face and ate eleven cupcakes."

"That was seven cupcakes," I said just before he kissed me.

For a minute I thought bells were ringing inside my head, but the jangling persisted even when the kiss ended, until I heard footsteps overhead and Delaney called from the top of the stairs. "Ginger? Ginger Cameron — you down there?"

I smoothed my hair and hurried into the hallway. Who could be calling me here unless there was an emergency at home? Had my grandfather had another heart attack? Or maybe something had happened to Mama Kate.

Delaney yawned. "You can pick it up down there," she said.

Bailey stood beside me as I yanked the receiver from its cradle. "What is it, Ginger?" he asked. "Is anything wrong?"

But only silence answered my greeting. "Hello," I said again. "This is Ginger Cameron."

Bailey frowned. "What happened? They hang up?"

I shook my head. "Oh, he's there," I told him, "he's just not talking."

Chapter Thirteen

I woke to the smell of something wonderful, and looked out my window to see several people standing around a large black cooking pot while Rob stirred it with what looked like a boat paddle. The grass glittered with frost, and Rob wore a bulky turtleneck sweater and a knitted cap pulled over his ears, yet I didn't see a cloud in the sky. It was a perfect day for Brunswick stew, and for a few minutes I forgot the suspicious phone call I had received the night before.

"Do you think it's that same guy?" Bailey had asked. "The one you told me about?"

"I don't know who else it could be," I said. "But how does he know where I am?" Unless someone told him, I thought.

"Don't let him intimidate you," Bailey said. "No one can get to you here. Believe me, if he tries, he'll regret it!" And he kissed me good night at the top of the stairs without any interference from Dahlia Brown. My late aunt must have taken the night off. But this time the bells didn't ring.

The kitchen smelled of chicken and pork

that had been cooking since early morning. Sheri sat at the table crying as she peeled onions while Rob browned the beef over a wood fire behind the tavern before simmering the combined meats and broth together. I took a doughnut from the platter on the table and poured a cup of coffee. "What can I do to help?"

Sheri sniffed loudly. "Open those jars of tomatoes, I guess. He'll be ready for them next. He don't want the corn and vinegar yet, he says." She tossed onions into the food processor. "Hey, I wore your skirt to a party last night. Looked real good with my boots — thanks."

I pried the tops from what seemed like an awful lot of mason jars and dumped the contents into a large bowl. "You're welcome," I said, wiping my eyes.

"I thought I'd wear it again tomorrow with that green cape . . . if you don't mind. I'll take good care of them, I promise."

I said it would be all right. What else could I say? After all, I did make the girl an offer, and Sheri had become attached to the cape right away. Not too attached, I hoped, but I had to admit it did look good with her blond hair.

I took the bowl of tomatoes to Rob, glad of an excuse to tell him of my visit to Mama

Kate's. He had already heard about my phone call and repeated Bailey's question. "Do you think it was Gideon Foster?"

I stood back as he slid the tomatoes into the pot. "I didn't hear his voice, but Delaney said it was a man. I just hope he was calling long distance." I fanned the smoke away. "This smells wonderful! Where did you learn to make it?"

"My grandmama taught me; we made it every year — with Uncle Barney's help, of course."

"Uncle Bar —? Oh, your dog, you mean! And what did he do?"

Rob gave a wide stir with his paddle. "Chased the raccoons away." He glanced at Agnes curled on the sunny back step. "If that cat was worth even the tip of Uncle Barney's tail, she'd be out here earning her keep."

I laughed. "Well, don't expect me to take up his duties, although I wouldn't be surprised if I did start to bark or do something else strange. What comes after seeing ghosts?"

He stood back to listen while I told him about the letters. "Wonder if this Mason she mentions had anything to do with her death? Do you think Lucy might remember him?"

"Don't know, but I'll ask. And I want to find out about that necklace too — if I can do it without seeming obvious."

"Well, you won't have long to wait." Rob waved to the driver of a faded blue car that bumped to a stop by the old smokehouse, and Lucy Whitworth, in a rumpled gray sweat suit and tennis shoes, waved back.

"Promised I'd decorate the sanctuary for church tomorrow!" she called, stalking off into the brush. "You'd think I'd learn to keep my mouth shut by now!"

Rob turned to glare at Agnes, who had decided to investigate the pot. "Get away from here, you impudent animal! This is much too good for you." The cat, unperturbed, sat at his feet and feigned nonchalance. "I'm surprised the Methodist church is still operating," Rob said, watching Lucy wade off into the tall grass. "She's been gone for about six weeks now; I didn't think they knew how to get along without her." He laughed. "In fact, it's a wonder the town's still intact."

"She doesn't seem to be the bossy type," I said.

"Not bossy, just active. Lucy Whitworth can't sit still and do nothing; I'll bet she walks five miles a day! And whatever she decides to do, she does right." Rob looked up from his stirring and smiled. "Kind of like me."

"Sure," I said, and started inside. When I looked back, he had ladled a taste of stew on a magnolia leaf for Agnes. I pretended I didn't see.

I was helping Ethelene make sandwiches for lunch a little later when I heard a tapping from the back porch window and found Lucy mouthing words at me over an armload of bright foliage.

Ethelene cut crusts from a stack of wheat bread. "I think Rob's ready for the hot sauce and vinegar," she said. Obviously she was a better lip-reader than I was. I took the box from the pantry and hurried outside to find the porch littered with crimson sweetgum, russet sassafras, and the dark red stalks of sumac berries. Lucy, on her hands and knees, stuck them into tall earthenware jugs.

On my way back inside I stopped to admire them. "They're beautiful, Lucy! A florist couldn't have done better," I said, and meant it.

Lucy pulled a bramble out of her hair. "I like doing it — always have. I think people should stick with what they do best — that's why I stay out of the kitchen." She kicked debris from a spot on the steps.

"Stay a minute, can't you? Ethelene can spare you for a little while."

"You wanted to know about Dahlia," she began as I sat down. "Why?"

"Because I've seen her," I said. Why on earth did I tell her that? This woman was a stranger to me. I knew nothing about her except that she had been a friend of my aunt's. Or so she said.

I looked up, dreading to meet her eyes. I had probably scared her to death. But Lucy Whitworth made room for herself on the step beside me. "I thought you had," she said. "Where? The upstairs porch?"

I nodded. "In my room too. And the barn."

Then she did look surprised. A delayed reaction?

"You've seen her too?" I asked.

"Yes. Several times on the porch and once in the upstairs hall, but never in the barn. I don't even like to go out there." She twisted a strand of broom sage around her fingers and frowned. "The first time I thought I'd just imagined it — dreamed it or something. But when it happened again, it frightened me. I was afraid I was losing my mind . . . now I know better." She touched my arm lightly. "They're moving her grave, you know. Bailey tells me he finally located the family." Lucy propped her head on her hands and looked at me. "I wonder what it is that she wants. It must have something to do with the way she died." She looked down at her hands. "I don't think she has much time, Virginia."

"Your husband says you were the last one to see her. Do you remember what she had on?"

"It was the same dress she wore in the painting. They found her in it the next day."

"And the necklace?" I asked. "What about the necklace?"

"The coral necklace! Good Lord, I'd forgotten about that!" Lucy Whitworth clasped her knees and stared out at the pecan grove. "I think she . . . yes . . . I know she wore the necklace. There was a party that night, you see — a dance. Kirby and I left a little early." She smiled. "We were celebrating our engagement under that big elm that used to be out front, until Papa came out and made poor Kirby go home." She laughed. "I, of course, was sent to bed."

"So the last time you saw Dahlia Brown was at the party in the barn?"

She shook her head. "No, I didn't go up to bed right away. After Kirby went home I sat on the porch awhile. I was just going inside when I heard Chamblee and Dahlia whispering over by the trellis where the wisteria grew. I didn't want them to know I was listening, so I waited until he kissed her good night and left." Lucy brushed the chaff from her trousers. "She knew I was there all along! 'You can come out now, Lucy,' she said. So I did, and we sat out there and rocked for a while. Dahlia was quiet — for her — didn't talk much; said she had some thinking to do. Finally I went inside and left her there."

"Do you know what she was thinking about?"

"No, but she and my brother seemed to be getting kind of serious. I think he might have tried to get her to give up her acting and stay here."

"You said he kissed her good night and left," I reminded her. "Why would he leave? He lived here, didn't he?"

"Yes, but that was the summer Chamblee graduated from college. He had promised to help at the tavern until September, but by the end of August he was ready to get out — neither of us liked the hotel business, I'm afraid. Chamblee had a job interview with a newspaper the next day — had to drive half the night to get there."

"Where?" I asked.

She shrugged. "Some little town near Raleigh, I think."

How convenient, I thought. "By the way,"

I said as we carried the arrangements to her car. "Do you remember anyone named Mason living here that summer?"

She thought for a minute, then shook her head. "Mason? Mason who?"

"I don't know. Could've been a last name."

"No, I don't think so. Why?"

"Somebody mentioned it," I lied. "Maybe it was Ethelene or your brother. I know I've heard the name somewhere." I occupied myself by dusting off my hands. "Could it have been one of the actors?"

But Lucy Whitworth was firm. She didn't remember a Mason, and I thought she was telling the truth. But I wasn't sure.

We spent the early part of the afternoon setting long tables under a canopy on the lawn to hold the huge bowls of slaw that were taking up every inch of space in the big refrigerator — plus trays of bread and pickles. Even Delaney pitched in to help make the dark rich brownies we planned to serve for dessert. I wondered if Sam Molloy would show up for the picnic that afternoon, but I didn't dare ask.

Ethelene wasn't that shy. "Hadn't seen that good-looking young doctor around here lately," she said as we cut the last chocolaty batch into squares. She rubbed one narrow foot against the other and groaned. "You haven't scared him off, have you?"

Delaney fought with a roll of plastic wrap. "That depends on what you mean. I'm just not interested, that's all. The man's a workhorse."

"Thought you had more sense than that!" Ethelene muttered. "Some folks don't never learn.

"Ain't gonna be nothing left of them brownies if you eat 'em all," she said to me. "Why don't you do me a favor while there's still some left?"

I gulped the warm morsel that had broken apart from the rest, making sure I got the pecan that stuck to it. "Can I help it if they tear up? I'm eating only the messy ones."

"Yeah, well, that's the third one," Delaney reminded me.

I laughed. "But who's counting? Okay, what do you want me to do?" I asked Ethelene, washing my hands at the sink.

"Your car's out front, ain't it?" she asked.

I nodded.

"Well, once people start to pile in here, we'll need all the parking spaces we can get. You'll have to move it somewhere out back. Bailey says anywhere out past the pecan grove as long as it's out of the way.

"Good Lord, child! What's the matter with you?" she said to Delaney, who had a peculiar expression on her face. "You look like you just found out you was sittin' in church naked!"

"You're going to hate me, Ethelene. I just plain forgot." Delaney ran a hand loosely through her hair.

The housekeeper crossed her sturdy arms and frowned. "Forgot what?"

"The paper cups! I know you told me to pick them up from Otto, but it just went clean out of my head." Delaney punctuated her confession with a sigh.

She smiled, and I should have known what was coming. "Ginger, since you're going out to your car anyway, would you mind —"

"Give me credit for more sense than that," Ethelene said. "I had Bailey pick up the cups this morning; they're right there in the pantry. Might as well take them on out when you move your car."

"I'll get my keys," I said.

Never do anything for yourself if you can get somebody else to do it for you, I thought, backing out of my usual parking place. Delaney Davenport had fully intended that I run her errands for her — and I, being the obliging soul that I was, would have done it!

And then I forgot all about Delaney Davenport, the paper cups, and anything else but

153

trying to stay alive. Instead of making the wide turn around the corner of the house, my car continued to roll backward, and I didn't have any brakes.

Chapter Fourteen

I pumped frantically, but the brakes were useless. Behind me loomed the red and white striped awning where I had just left Sheri setting out dinnerware for the picnic. I was going to plow right through the middle of it! My foot came down so hard on the emergency pedal, I felt the jolt clear to my jaw, but the car didn't slow. Somebody yelled *stop* — as if I had a choice — and I pressed on the horn to warn them, then swung the wheel to the left. Something crunched and scraped as a back tire bumped over it . . . I think I shut my eyes.

When I opened them, the canopy rushed past in a peppermint blur about six inches from my front fender, then the car lurched, jarring every internal organ in my body before it ricocheted into something with a loud, splintering crack.

It took me a while to grasp the fact that I was no longer moving and still alive. A harsh, annoying sound vibrated all around me, and I wished whoever was doing it would stop.

I looked up to see Rob pulling open my door. "Ginger, you can take your hand off the horn now. . . . Ginger, are you all right?" He touched my cheek with a warm hand that smelled of wood smoke. "Maybe you'd better just sit there a minute. Do you hurt anywhere? Somebody call Sam Molloy!"

A woman screamed hysterically. Sheri. I don't know if she was crying for my near escape or her own; both, maybe. I took the hand Rob offered and climbed out onto the solid, reliable ground that had seemed so treacherous a minute before. "I'm okay, really," I said to his repeated inquiries. "Just a little dizzy, that's all."

Somebody shoved a chair beneath me, and I felt a firm hand on my head and a cold, damp towel on the back of my neck. "Take a deep breath, honey," Ethelene said, and I did. I was glad she was there. "You had a close one that time," she added. "Lord, I'm glad Rob didn't dig up that old quince bush like he wanted to. It hasn't bloomed in three years."

I glanced at the shrub in question. It certainly wasn't going to bloom now. It was as flat as my current bank account. I had also bumped over the stone border of what had once been a flower bed before smashing into a small tree, now bent and shattered beneath my car.

"Mama had that little red bud planted there just before she left," Delaney announced, inspecting the wreckage.

"I'm glad," I said.

"My God, I'm as limp as a dishrag! What happened?" Sheri still sniffed. If her eyes weren't so red, she wouldn't have a bit of color in her face. "I didn't think you were going to stop."

"Neither did I," I told her. "My brakes are gone. If that little tree hadn't been there, I guess I'd still be going."

Rob brought me a glass of water. I would have preferred something a little stronger. "When's the last time you used your car?" he asked.

"Not since I got back last night." There was so much to do around Plumb-Nelly during weekends, I didn't have time to go anywhere else. If Ethelene hadn't asked me to move my car, I probably wouldn't have found out about the brakes until I started to work on Monday . . . *down Oh My God Boulevard!* I always parked my car near the house at the top of the hill. If I had turned in the other direction, there would have been nothing to stop me. I reached for her hand. "You did me a favor," I said. "I could be wrapped around that tree down at the bend."

And then I remembered Delaney's asking me to go for the cups. It must have occurred to her, too, because she came and stood beside my chair, dark hair disheveled from her constant tugging. "I guess I ought to thank you too," she said to Ethelene. "Ginger, I'm so glad you're not hurt!"

Bailey seemed to be pleased about it as well — after he got over the shock of seeing my car impaled on a sapling. He had been to The Store for beer and ice, and when he rounded the curve to the backyard, he stopped so suddenly, I expected his car to stand on end. At least he appeared to be relieved to see me sitting there with all my limbs intact, although he couldn't be as happy about it as I was.

"Ginger!" He made his way through the circle around me. "What on earth happened to your car?"

I told him, and he looked appropriately distraught. I couldn't remember having so much attention, and I was beginning to kind of enjoy it.

"You aren't hurt?" He looked at my car and wondered, I'm sure, why I wasn't hanging off a limb somewhere. "Do you want me to call Sam?"

"No, don't — please. Except for the feeling

that my insides played a game of fruit basket-turnover, I'm okay. For a while I felt like my liver and lungs had switched places, and my heart just shot clean out of my chest and hasn't come back yet!" I laughed. He didn't.

"Well, I'm calling Bud Grady right now. We'll find out exactly what caused this."

"Who's Bud Grady?"

Bailey frowned as though I hadn't been listening at all. "Owns Grady's Garage!" Silly me, I should have known. He bent over me to whisper, "Take it easy now; you've had a bad scare. Delaney and I will fill in for you."

"Does this chair come with a seat belt?" Delaney said. "Maybe we should fasten you in for safekeeping." She smiled when she said it, but I don't think she was overjoyed about working my shift. At least she wouldn't have much serving to do, I thought, as everyone would help themselves today.

"How about a tall, cool one?" Rob appeared beside me with a bottle in his hand.

"A beer would be great," I told him. "What's that, Worcestershire sauce?"

"This goes in the stew, silly. Bailey's icing down the beer in that big tub over there. Why don't you let me move your chair for you? You can keep me company while I stir. I promise you won't have to get up again."

That sounded good to me, and I took him up on it — for the better part of an hour. But when the yard started to fill with people, I found they were not only hungry but curious, and I had to repeat my story so many times, I began to wish I'd taped it. When Bud Grady came with his wrecker to tow my car away, it seemed as if the questions would start a new rotation.

The appearance of Grace Millsap weaving her way through the crowd gave me the inspiration I needed, and I found I could walk as well as ever. Run if I had to. Intending to hide in the kitchen, I hurried toward the house. I was halfway across the yard when she called to me.

"Don't run away, now!" she said, trying her best to smile. "I know you didn't mean to spill that coffee, and Dr. Sam says it shouldn't even leave a scar."

"I'm glad," I said, putting my tongue on hold. I didn't care if she had a scar as big as Alaska.

"Since you're going inside, how about bringing me one of those porch pillows to sit on? Those old chairs get as hard as last week's corn bread after a while, and my back just hasn't been right since that —"

"I'll be happy to," I said, leaving her in mid-whine. I waved to her from the back porch. "Be right back!"

I spent at least fifteen minutes in the kitchen helping Delaney slice lemons for tea before I returned with the pillow, hoping she had given up waiting. No such luck: Graceless, as Rob called her, paced in obvious exasperation at the foot of the steps. "What kept you?" she asked, jerking the pillow from my hand. "My back's near about give out standing here waiting."

"Sorry. I had to give Ethelene a hand in the kitchen. Why don't you sit down, Mrs. Millsap, and I'll get you a glass of tea?" Then leave the county if necessary, I thought. But Sheri, looking a little shaky and subdued, chose that moment to offer a tray of drinks and foiled my escape.

"You were asking about that girl," Grace Millsap said, indicating the empty chair beside her. "That redheaded actress with the funny name?" She took a dainty sip of tea. "Had her cap set for Chamblee Davenport, no two ways about it. Tried to get in good with his sister, too, but she couldn't fool that Lucy!"

"What do you mean? Lucy's husband, Kirby, told me the two of them were good friends." And so did Lucy Whitworth herself, but I wasn't going to tell her that.

"Well, of course he would! That's what he

wanted everybody to think." She beckoned me closer and whispered into her cup. "Let me tell you, there wasn't a man around that woman didn't flirt with! Why, for a while she was after Kirby as well — and him as good as engaged to Lucy Davenport!" Grace crunched on a piece of ice and smiled. "Guess she thought Chamblee had more money."

"What woman? You mean Dahlia Brown?"

"Well, of course! Who else?"

"What makes you think that?"

"Because it's the truth, that's why, and you can take my word for it." She rolled her eyes. "Well, Lucy Davenport put a stop to that."

"She did?" Uh-oh! Rob looked as if he were about to come over, and I gave him a fierce look to discourage him. I smiled at Grace. "How?"

"Oh, I heard them arguing; Lucy just plain lost her temper! Said she didn't see how Dahlia could do such a thing, and what could she be thinking of? I tell you, they got into it right hot and heavy."

"Really? And what did Dahlia have to say?"

"Said what she did was her own business and she didn't want to hear any more about it. But Lucy had the final word. She told that actress there were some things you just didn't do, and if she didn't know that by now, it was time she learned. When Lucy started to cry I got out of there! I was afraid they'd find me listening — not that I meant to, you know, but I was passing their door with the dust mop and couldn't help but hear what they said."

"No, of course not," I said. That had to have been the shiniest spot in the hallway.

"Do you remember anyone here named Mason that summer?" I asked. "One of the actors maybe?"

She gave me such a puzzled look, I thought at first she hadn't understood. "Mason?" she said finally. "Mason. My heavens, how would I know? That's been a long time, you know. Surely you don't expect me to remember everybody who stayed here!"

Grace Millsap was silent for a minute, and I was just about to sneak quietly away when she grasped me by the arm. "I always wondered how that woman came to die like she did. She didn't seem the sort to be wandering around at night — unless she was with somebody she trusted."

"I think Rob's getting ready to serve the stew," I said, excusing myself. "I'd better go and see if he needs some help." I hurried across the lawn and stood over the embers from the cooking fire, glad for the warmth. Was the woman implying that Bailey's aunt had been responsible for Dahlia's death?

When supper was served I picked a spot as far away from Grace as I could with Eugenia on one side, and Mercer Belle Abernathy a large cushiony barrier on the other. The comfortable sound of people talking, and the rich, smoky smell of the stew lulled me into believing for just a little while that everything was all right at Plumb-Nelly Tavern. The Brunswick stew was hot enough to melt metal and the best I'd ever eaten. I looked for Rob so I could give my compliments to the chef, but he had taken a well-earned break. When Bailey offered to bring me another bowl, I accepted without a second thought and didn't even leave enough for a dog to lick.

The sun was going down, and an owl called from some where beyond the pecan grove as we finished our dessert. The group began to break up as people started to feel the chill and drift away. I was glad when Lucy and Kirby Whitworth joined our circle and the easy flow of chatter continued. I wasn't ready for the feeling to end. Finally Kirby yawned. "Well, the deep of night is crept upon our talk, and nature must obey . . ." he said. Bailey stood behind me with a hand on my shoulder, and his aunt Lucy was entertaining us with a funny story about some tourists she had met on her trip, when Sheri called me from the back porch.

"Ginger! Can you come to the phone, or do you want me to tell him to call back?"

Him. I glanced at Bailey. Even before I went inside I knew there would be no one there.

Chapter Fifteen

It occurred to me as I hurried through the dim back hallway that it could be my stepfather calling about an advertising account on the paper back home, or perhaps someone working late at *The Bugle*. But the same threatening silence greeted me when I answered the phone, and I clenched the receiver, wishing it were the caller's throat. Don't let him get to you, I told myself. And for God's sake, don't let him know it! "I'm afraid you have the wrong number," I said calmly before hanging up the phone.

I looked up to see Bailey and Eugenia standing in the doorway to the parlor. Bailey didn't even have to ask. When he looked at me he knew. "I'm calling Bud at the garage," he said, reaching for the telephone. "I don't like this worth a damn!"

Eugenia followed me into the kitchen, where I mechanically put away the leftover brownies and stored the remainder of the tea in the refrigerator. "You might as well tell me about it now," she said, sitting ramrod-straight in a kitchen chair. "I'm not going to leave you alone till you do.

"Do you think this Gideon is somewhere around here?" she asked when I told her.

"I hope not, but apparently he knows where I am."

Her red nails pecked the tabletop. "I don't want to alarm you, Virginia, but has it occurred to you that he could be responsible for what happened to your car?"

"I've already thought of that." Bailey let the door swing shut behind him. "I finally got Bud Grady at home. He hasn't had a chance to check your car thoroughly, Ginger, but he did find a loose bleed screw."

I wiped a smudge of slaw from the countertop. "A loose what?"

"Bleed screw. It's a valve controlling the flow of brake fluid to the hydraulic system. If only one of them gets loose enough, the fluid can leak out. He thinks that's probably what happened."

Bailey frowned. "The thing is, it would be hard to tell if it just wasn't tight enough in the first place or if somebody helped it along."

Sheri stood in the doorway with an empty tea pitcher in each hand. "You mean somebody actually *did something* to your car? They meant for that to happen?" Her bright lipstick made her small face look even whiter.

"And I think I know when they did it," Eugenia said, pounding the table with a final slap. "I don't always sleep so well when I've drunk too much coffee, and last night was one of those nights. My room overlooks that side of the house, you know, and along about two or three in the morning I thought I heard something down there, but I didn't think too much about it. Figured it was just Delaney coming home late, or maybe a raccoon after the garbage."

"Wouldn't the fluid leave a puddle?" I asked.

As if on cue, the four of us filed outside. By the yellow glow of the porch light we could see the oily stain on the gravel where my car had been. I picked up a pebble and sniffed it. It had a strong smell.

"You didn't happen to hear anything, did you?" I asked Sheri. I knew she had stayed at Plumb-Nelly the night before so she and Rob could get an early start on the stew, and had heard her moving about in the room next to mine.

"You got up to check on the pork, didn't you, Sheri?" Bailey asked. "Did you notice anything then?"

But the girl shook her head. "In the middle of the night? I was too sleepy." She yawned.

"Look, I'll see you tomorrow, okay? I've got to get home to bed."

I heard footsteps behind us and turned to see Rob coming from the back of the house. "What happened? Somebody lose a contact?" he asked.

I showed him the brake fluid and told him what Bud Grady had said. "I got another call tonight," I said. "Bailey thinks Gideon might have tampered with my car."

Rob wiped a smutty sleeve across his face, leaving a black smear. He looked rumpled and tired, and I could see he was trying to keep from yawning, but he put a friendly arm across my shoulders as we walked back inside. "Have you called the police?" he asked Bailey.

Bailey shook his head. "I doubt if there's anything they could do about it tonight, but I'll call them first thing tomorrow."

The wide entrance hall seemed safe and well lit with all the lights burning, and Bailey double-bolted the massive front door behind us. "Try not to worry, Ginger; nobody's going to get in here tonight. They'd be a fool to try."

He was right, of course, I thought as I stood in the shower, letting the hot water pound me. Bailey had left on the outside lights and the tavern's thick doors were secure. Besides, Gideon had never hurt me, had never even suggested it. Surely he wouldn't come here! But what if whoever was doing this was already inside?

When I woke later I thought that Agnes, who had gone to sleep on my window seat, was scratching to get out. But the cat still slept undisturbed, and I crawled to the foot of the bed and stretched over her dark mound of fur to see what was going on. Delaney laughed somewhere below me, and as I looked, hooked her partner's arm in hers and swung around in kind of a predawn dos-a-dos. Two dark silhouettes against a smoky morning background, they gradually made their way up the brick walk to the back steps almost beneath my window. After a few minutes of mumbled conversation I heard the screen door shut and was getting ready to worm under the covers, when I spotted the man start back across the yard.

Before he moved into the shadows I saw the shape of his elegant head — the hair cut and styled to give one the impression he was born with it looking that way. I had even been a little jealous that it always looked better than mine. I recognized the jacket — the oh-so-casual khaki jacket that swung when he walked and that he flipped aside when he stooped to get into his car. And for a second, as he drove out from under the dark screen of trees, I saw a flash of red.

"How do you tell somebody they're dating a lunatic?" I asked Rob as we went down to breakfast the next morning. "I can't imagine where Delaney met up with this creep — or what she sees in him, for that matter."

He just looked at me and grinned. "How long did you date him, Ginger? He must have appealed to you for a while." He stopped me before we reached the landing. "Look, are you sure this guy is Gideon? You said yourself it was dark."

I stepped ahead of him, shoving his hand aside. "No, I'm not sure it was Gideon! He just looked like him, moved like him, and dressed like him. And he was driving a red sports car. Do I have to get his blood type?"

"Well, that does it, Virginia Cameron! I'm calling the wedding off. And I had all eight of our children named too." He stood on the step above me, looking so offended I almost believed him. "Beware the scourge of a sharp-tongued woman!" And he raised a wall-like palm between us. In the corridor below I thought I heard Bailey's door close softly.

I giggled. "Since it's Sunday, I think I'll go to church and count my blessings," I said.

171

"*Eight,* did you say?" I was still laughing as we walked into the dining room. I didn't laugh long.

"There's an envelope for you on the desk," Eugenia said, looking up from her coffee. "Did you see it?"

"No, where?"

"In the entrance hall. One of those big manila envelopes — right on top. Had your name on it."

"But there's no mail today. I wonder how it —" I looked at Rob. He wasn't smiling anymore. "Do you know how it got there, Eugenia?"

"It was there when I came down. Chamblee probably brought it over — could be something to do with the paper." Eugenia nibbled at a muffin. I don't think she even convinced herself.

I balled my fingers into a fist to keep my hand from trembling as I reached for the packet. I wasn't going to allow this man to turn me into a basket case! Rob stood close beside me as I opened the flap and drew out two glossy photographs. One was of Rob and me talking beside the flower bed as I was getting ready to leave for Mama Kate's. The other, taken a day or so earlier, showed me walking with Bailey from the restaurant the night we went to the play. "Dammit all!" I said, and started to rip them down the middle.

"Hey, don't do that!" Rob snatched them away. "You don't want to destroy the evidence." He tucked them under his arm. "Come on, let's find out if Bailey has gotten in touch with the police."

Frowning politely, Bailey looked up at our knock. A large textbook of some kind lay open on the desk in front of him. "Have you talked with the police yet?" I asked.

Bailey took a swallow from his coffee mug. "Not yet. I was waiting for you to come down — in case they had any questions."

Rob held out the photographs. "They might be interested in these."

"Good Lord! Where did these come from?"

"That's what we're trying to find out. Eugenia says they were on the front desk when she came downstairs for breakfast." Rob examined them over his shoulder. "Actually, that's not a bad picture of me. Ginger's frowning a little though . . . sun must have been in your face."

I decided to ignore him. "We have to talk with Delaney," I told Bailey. "I think I know how the pictures got here. She was with Gideon last night."

She denied it, of course. "His name is Al

Cline, and I doubt if he's ever heard of you, Ginger! Why, he's not even from Florida."

"How do you know?" I asked.

"Well . . . he told me. Al came down here from Ohio. And he's not a photographer; he's a sales representative for a computer company."

Rob nodded. "We buy an awful lot of computers here in Fiddler's Glen," he said with a perfectly straight face.

"Never mind that!" Bailey faced his sister across the cluttered desk. "Did he give you this envelope?"

Delaney only glanced at it. "The one with Ginger's name on it? Yes, he found it on the floor by the back door."

"Did you actually see it there?" her brother persisted.

"Well, no, but I saw him pick it up." Delaney glared at me. "Why are you doing this, Ginger? Why is everyone so dead set against my having a little fun?"

She seemed to behaving more than a little fun last night, I thought; and I doubted if she could remember how her companion had come to have the manila envelope. "Well, it looks like I'll just have to prove it!" she said finally. "Will it make you happy if I call him?"

But "Al Cline" wasn't at the number he'd

given her. In fact, the people at the motel had never heard of him.

Delaney wouldn't have anything to do with me for the rest of the day, which made it kind of difficult with both of us helping in the dining room with the after-church crowd. Eugenia caught on right away, of course, entertaining herself at our expense. "Delaney, would you ask Virginia to pour me some coffee, please?" Or, "Virginia, be so kind as to tell Delaney my room was a little cool last night."

It was more than a little cool as Delaney and I cleared the long tables, and the clatter of dishes and cutlery only accentuated the silence between us. Sheri claimed an upset stomach and left early after moping around all morning, but not before she borrowed my cape for her date that night.

I don't know what Delaney told the local policeman who came by that afternoon. A slight, soft-spoken man with an amazing appetite for Ethelene's pumpkin bread, Ron Slater spoke to us privately in the front parlor before calling us together.

"It looks like this Al Cline, or Gideon — if that's who it is — has cleared out," he told us. "And from what Bud tells me, we have no way of knowing if he or anyone else drained your brake fluid. I'll have them run a check on him tomorrow and let you know if there's anything to go on." He smiled a sad little smile, as if he were apologizing in advance for what he didn't expect to find. "Of course you know there's not much we can do unless this harassment takes a mean turn," he said to me. "You will let us know if you hear from him again?"

I agreed. From the casual way he spoke, I didn't believe he considered Gideon a serious threat. The phone calls and photographs were a nuisance, but a harmless one, and I had the distinct impression that he thought me a bit neurotic. Maybe I was.

When the telephone rang just after dark I picked it up without even thinking, and the words came like a blow to the stomach. This time Gideon didn't even pretend.

"Ginger, we need to talk," he said as if we had just parted after a friendly tiff.

I gripped the receiver and looked around for help. Delaney was upstairs brooding and Rob and Bailey were off somewhere on errands of their own.

"Can you meet me in the meadow? You know, the one they call Fiddler's Meadow — across from that little white church. Ginger, please! I have to see you."

It was all I could do to keep from screaming, *Sure, and why don't you hold your breath until I get there?* But I had been warned not to answer.

I replaced the receiver without saying a word, pleased — and a little surprised — at my self-control, but not before I heard his final words.

"I'll be waiting," Gideon said.

I phoned the local police and left a message for Ron Slater to call, then sat for a long time in the darkness at the top of the stairs. The devil would be skiing around hell in his long johns before I'd willingly be alone with Gideon Foster!

Chapter Sixteen

The next morning a neighbor, out for her daily walk, heard a faint whimpering under the bridge in Fiddler's Meadow, and discovered Sheri Griffin almost hidden by bushes beside the shallow creek. Barely conscious, the girl was badly bruised and had suffered a serious head injury.

Ethelene, who brought us the news, sat at the kitchen table dabbing at her eyes with a pink flowered handkerchief. "They've taken her to the hospital," she said, easing out of her shoes, "but it don't sound good . . . it don't sound good at all." And abandoning all pretense of composure, she cried her way through the handkerchief and three paper napkins.

Rob stood with his hands on her shoulders and looked beseechingly at me, but I didn't know what to say either. "Do they know how it happened?" I asked. "How long had she been there?"

"All night, it seems," Ethelene said. "Her bed hadn't been slept in. Her mama thought she was spending the night with a girlfriend."

I held to the edge of the scarred oak table. "Do you know what she was wearing?"

Ethelene shook her head. "Why? Does it matter?"

One look at Rob told me we were thinking the same thing.

"Yes, I'm afraid it does matter," I said, sitting a little too suddenly in the hard chair. "Whoever did this to Sheri probably thought it was me." I was glad I hadn't had breakfast, because I don't think I would have kept it. I put my face in my hands and closed my eyes. It was my fault Sheri was hurt. And if she died, that would be my fault too.

As I explained to Ethelene about Gideon, Bailey came in from the hallway, where he had been talking on the phone with the police. "Sheri's still alive," he said, obviously trying to be encouraging in spite of the grim look in his eyes. "But she can't tell them much." With long strides he crossed to the sink and filled a glass with water, then stood with it in his hand. "A car came upon her while she was on the bridge, but from what they could gather, all she saw were the headlights."

I stared fascinated at the way the sunlight struck the clear water in the glass. It would be nice to let it hypnotize me, to go away somewhere. . . . "The cape. Was she wearing the cape?"

Absently he set the glass aside. "It was twisted around her. Police are checking with authorities in Shell City, Ginger. If it's Gideon, we'll know something soon."

"I have to know now!" I stood, almost knocking my chair backward. "I'm going to call home." If I had done this sooner, I thought, waiting for my stepfather to come on the line, maybe Sheri wouldn't be lying there in the hospital. But I had to admit to myself that I really hadn't wanted to know.

I wasn't surprised when Haynes Reinhold told me he didn't know where Gideon was. "He hasn't been doing any work for us lately, but I thought he'd just given up free-lancing," he told me. "Look, give me a few minutes and I'll ask around and call you back." I heard the squeak of his chair, the tapping of his pencil on the desk. "Ginger, what's wrong? He hasn't been calling again, has he?"

I told him about the photographs and the phone calls, then explained what had happened to Sheri. "It was supposed to have been me," I said. "She was wearing my cape, and he's conceited enough to think I would meet him there. It has to be Gideon!"

"Well, looks like he's cleared out," he said when he called back a few minutes later. "I got a recording that says his phone's been disconnected, and nobody around here's seen him for several weeks." Haynes sighed and I could picture him rubbing the furrows on his brow as if he could erase them. "The police here warned him about getting in touch with you — told me to let them know if there was a problem . . . you have spoken to the authorities there about this, Virginia? My God! When your mother hears —"

"Then don't tell her! Please, Haynes. It isn't going to help. And the police do know; in fact, they're supposed to meet me at the newspaper this morning, so I'd better run. I'll keep in touch, I promise."

During the short drive to *The Bugle* I thought of Sheri as she must have looked when they found her — dirty and bleeding, lying twisted on the ground. Poor, vain little Sheri! How she would hate being seen like that. By now Gideon must know he had run down the wrong person. I would be next.

Ron Slater had gone off his shift a few minutes earlier when I called the night before and hadn't gotten my message until after Sheri was found. If he had, would it have made a difference? Bailey had told me the police wanted to ask me some questions about Gideon's last call, and I found them waiting when I pulled into the newspaper's small parking lot.

Chamblee Davenport graciously gave up his office so that we could have privacy, and I found myself sitting across from Ron Slater, the same gentle-voiced policeman who had seemed dubious about my concerns the day before. "Now," he began, waiting for his slow smile to sink in — to ease me, I assumed. "We've learned this Gideon Foster has gone from that town in Florida without leaving any forwarding address, so he might very well be in this vicinity." He leaned back in Chamblee's swivel chair. "However, we don't know if he's the person who did that to Sheri Griffin last night.

"You are absolutely sure that was Gideon Foster who called you?" He shifted in his seat, threaded a pencil through stubby fingers.

I didn't answer. I was absolutely sure where I'd like to tell him to put that pencil, but I was going to be good if it killed me. Keep your mouth shut, Virginia, I told myself.

He got my message anyway. I think. He smiled at me again, and this time I smiled back. "Who knew he was expecting you to meet him at the bridge?" he asked.

I had said something to Bailey and Rob — and to Mrs. T.S.S. of course, I told him.

He frowned. "Mrs. who?"

"Eugenia. Eugenia Tyler Stafford-Smith."

182

I shrugged. "I just call her Mrs. T.S.S."

The policeman laughed. "I don't blame you. Would any of them have mentioned this to someone else, do you think? Are you sure no one overheard? You know how people are always milling about at Plumb-Nelly — in and out all the time."

"But not on Sunday night. We don't serve on Sunday nights. The only people who drop by then are usually —"

"Family," he said, tossing the pencil aside. "And were any there last night?"

I had to think. Lucy Whitworth had brought over one of the large arrangements she'd used in the church. "Seems a shame to go to all that trouble for just one day," she'd said, setting it down in the entrance hall. I couldn't remember how long she'd stayed after that. Long enough to give Bailey a breezy kiss. To chat briefly with Eugenia. I tried not to make a face when he wrote that down.

"Anyone else?" he said.

"Delaney. But she stayed upstairs most of the evening." Sulking — but I didn't tell him that. Another point for being good. "And Otto Millsap dropped by with his mother for a few minutes. Said she'd left her purse there the night before."

He raised an eyebrow. "And had she?"

"We didn't find it."

"I'd like to know how this character knew you were here," he said. "Aren't your whereabouts supposed to be a secret?"

I had thought of that. "It must have happened when Mom forwarded my mail. Whenever I get letters from friends, she just writes the new address on the front and sends them on. She probably put them in the mailbox out front for the postman to pick up. Anyone could have come up on the porch when she wasn't looking."

I followed him to the door when the interview was over. "You will let us know about Sheri, won't you? I can't imagine what she was doing on that bridge!"

He turned and gave me a frankly curious look. "Waiting for her boyfriend, I reckon."

"But why the bridge? Why didn't he come to her house?"

"Same reason she told her mama she was staying with a friend. She didn't want her to know she was seeing him." He shook his head at me and ambled across the road to his car.

"Who?" I yelled after him. "Who was she supposed to meet?" But he didn't answer.

"I'll tell you who," Ethelene said at noon as I helped her pile squares of hot corn bread in napkin-lined baskets. That and vegetable soup would have to do, she announced. And them that didn't like it could go elsewhere.

"It was that sorry Leonard Wardlaw — Henry Wardlaw's boy. Lives over near Stony Point somewhere. Never saw one of them Wardlaws yet who could tell the truth or hold his liquor!" Ethelene tossed the empty pan in the sink. "Done been married twice and run around on both of them. I don't blame Louise Griffin — Louise, that's Sheri's mama — for not wanting her to see him. You see where it's gotten her, don't you?"

"You don't think Leonard had anything to do with what happened, do you?" I put the baskets on a tray, hoping she would say he had. At least it wouldn't be my fault.

But Ethelene shot down my hopes with one long, hissing syllable that I had learned not only meant no, but that she was too disgusted to talk about it. Much. "Said she never showed up. She was supposed to meet him at Bennie's Grill; when she didn't come, he went home with that blond waitress there. Folks there back him up. Leonard Wardlaw wasn't even near here last night!"

I didn't ask her where she got her information. It wouldn't do to question Ethelene's sources. Besides, they usually turned out to be infallible.

Only a few regulars came for lunch that day. I guess they realized we would be short-handed as well as jittery after what happened to Sheri. Chamblee had sent me home early from *The Bugle*. "I can handle the ads better than I can wait on tables," he'd said. "For a few days at least."

Delaney took time off from her shop to help out too, although she made it known (especially to me) it was the prime sacrifice. When Sam Molloy showed up for his usual thirty-minute lunch break, I made sure she waited on his end of the table. Maybe he would supply an antivenin for the poisonous looks she gave me.

Eugenia sat alone, crumbling corn bread into her soup. Her friend Mercer Belle had left for home earlier, and she looked so lonely I slipped into the chair across from her. She glanced up and gave me a mournful look. "Don't suppose they've heard from Sheri?"

"Not yet," I said.

"Well, she's a silly little thing, but she's always been kind to me. I hope she makes it, but it doesn't seem likely."

I chose that moment to cry, of course, and poor Eugenia didn't know quite what to say or do. Finally she leaned over the table, almost dunking her large bosom in the soup. "Oh, dear Lord, Virginia! I'm awfully sorry. I didn't mean to upset you

. . . sometimes I haven't a bit of sense!"

"It's all right . . . not your fault . . ." I wiped my eyes on a napkin. "It's just that I know that was meant to be me."

Eugenia narrowed her eyes at me. "What do you mean?"

"She was wearing my cape. I was supposed to meet Gideon there last night. Remember?"

"Bosh!" Eugenia said. "If that's what's worrying you, forget it. Sheri wasn't hurt because she was wearing your cape. Somebody wanted her out of the way."

"Why?"

"Knew something she oughtn't, that's why."

"Oh, come on, Eugenia! Knew what? This is Sheri Griffin we're talking about, remember?"

Eugenia took a gulp of her coffee. "I've known that girl a lot longer than you have, Virginia. Sheri tells the truth only when it suits her; for heaven's sake, her own mother thought she was spending the night with a girlfriend!"

"But what does that have to do with me?"

I watched, fascinated, as Eugenia's heavy gold locket swung from one mountainous breast to the other. She took a deep breath and fastened in on me with those bright black

187

eyes. "Remember yesterday when we were talking about the intruder I heard — the one who drained your brake fluid?"

I nodded, eager for her to get on with it. "Well, Sheri said she was too sleepy to notice when she went down to check on the pork . . . but she was lying."

"How do you know?" I looked about. Otto Millsap held up a coffee cup, trying to get my attention.

"Take my word for it, I just know," Eugenia said. "Sheri Griffin saw somebody outside that night, and that's why she ended up under that bridge in Fiddler's Meadow."

Chapter Seventeen

"The freezer's off key today," Rob remarked as we loaded the dishwasher after lunch.

Three other people were in the kitchen and three people stared at him.

"Haven't you ever noticed? It hums in B flat, but it's not quite with it today."

"Neither am I," Delaney said, throwing her apron at a chair on her way out the door. "I'll be at the shop if anybody wants me."

Ethelene scalded her big soup pot and turned it upside down to dry. "You two go on and get out of here! This is about all we can do until time to start dinner. Get out in the sunshine, get some air." She sat down to lace up her shoes. "If it weren't for these old feet, I'd walk up into those hills myself."

I looked at Rob. "Let's do it! Can you get away?" In spite of what Eugenia had said, I still felt certain Sheri had been mistaken for me. I needed some repose.

"I have a better idea," he said. "Do you ride?"

"Assuming you mean horses — not since college, why?"

"Pete Barnwell down the road raises walking horses, and he's always glad to have somebody take them out. There's an easy trail that winds up into the foothills if you want to go. We should be back in a couple of hours."

"Just give me a minute to change," I said, and hurried upstairs to put on jeans; since the afternoons were sometimes brisk, I pulled on a sweater over my shirt.

Lucy Whitworth was getting out of her car as Rob and I walked outside, and she looked so sad — almost a negative of her usual cheerful self — that I thought she might have heard bad news from the hospital. But Lucy shook her head, hesitating for a minute on the flagstone walk. "No, as far as I know she's just the same. Thought I'd stop by and offer my services to Ethelene . . . not that I can cook, but I can dish up food, I guess — carry trays."

"That would be great," I said. Maybe she could take Delaney's place. "We should be back in plenty of time to help." I told her about the trail ride.

"I have just the horse picked out for Ginger," Rob said. "Name's Beelzebub."

Lucy smiled for the first time. "Well, that seems appropriate for a ride through Devil's Bluff. We used to ride there when I was younger, take picnics and stay all day. Wish I could go with you now."

"We'll wait," Rob offered, "if you want to come along."

"That horse would dump me before we'd gone a mile! It's been too long now. Couldn't get anybody around here to ride with me. Kirby used to, but he says he's getting too old; Delaney's always busy, and Bailey had one run away with him when he was a child and hasn't been easy on a horse since." She touched my arm. "But don't tell him I told you that."

"Frankly I'm glad to hear it," Rob admitted. "He puts me away at tennis, and last summer I saw him swim the river in what looked like about five strokes."

"Never mind that," I said. "What is this about Devil's Bluff? I thought you said this trail was easy."

"Oh, that's just the name they gave it," Lucy explained. "Because of the fiddler, you know. He was supposed to have ridden through there that night."

Rob grinned. "Still does. Some say they can hear the hoofbeats, and if you listen real good —"

"Will you hush that! You'll frighten Ginger so she'll refuse to ride with you, and I don't blame her. Devil's Bluff is only a gentle hill," she explained. "Dahlia and I used to go there whenever we could get away. She'd never been on a horse before she came here, but she was a natural rider. That ridge over there between those two hills is where they think she fell."

"What do you think happened?" I asked.

"I don't know, Virginia. And God help me, I don't want to know." Lucy Whitworth turned and hurried into the house.

The stable was only a few minutes drive from Plumb-Nelly, but by the time we got there I wasn't so sure I wanted to ride at all. "This horse — its name isn't really Beelzebub, is it?" I asked. "Look, I am not riding any animal who doesn't have my welfare at heart. Do you understand?"

"Obviously you aren't aware of the horse's lineage, Virginia." Rob appraised me with what I'm sure he considered a cool stare. "Beelzebub was sired by Mister Malicious out of Galloping Tornado. You won't get a more challenging mount than that."

"Oh, go away!" I stared him down until he finally gave in and laughed. "Bring me a horse named Buttercup or Grannie Grunt or something, or you can call yourself the lone Ranger, Rob Quillian!"

The horse he led out for me was a dirty

white with brown mane and tail and her name, I learned, was Sally Gray. After she discovered I wasn't going to let her nibble on every blade of grass in the meadow, we got along just fine.

The grazing land was still green, and we rode through dusty Queen Anne's lace, goldenrod, and silvery rabbit tobacco until we came to the woodlands, where each bright-tinged leaf seemed to stand out separate from the others. Once in a while through the trees I caught a glimpse of sky: a bright blue sky with little rabbit-tail clouds here and there. It didn't seem a place where bad things could happen, but they had happened. My aunt's body had been found here, they said, and now someone had tried to kill Sheri.

The trees thinned some as we began to climb, and when we reached a plateau, Rob, who had gone ahead, waited for me to join him. We tied the horses to a limb and climbed onto a rock where we could look down on the valley below. "That must be where they found your aunt," Rob said, pointing to a narrow ravine. "It doesn't make any sense, does it? Why would she be wandering around up here alone in the dark? She couldn't have been on a horse — not dressed the way she was."

He shrugged. "If Lucy Whitworth doesn't know, I guess nobody does."

"Mason does," I reminded him. "Whoever he is. Or was. Somehow, I've got to find him."

"How do you know he's still around here? Or alive?" Rob held out a hand to help me over a rock. "And even if you find him, we don't know that he had anything to do with your aunt's death."

"And we also don't know he didn't." I followed him hopscotch-style over the stones across a small stream and felt cold water ooze into my shoe. "If only she could talk!"

"Who?"

"Dahlia Brown. Why can't she just tell us who killed her? It would make it a lot easier."

"Maybe she doesn't know," he said.

"Ethelene says she heard the fiddler — the ghost fiddler, like that girl in the story, but I can't believe she'd follow the music all the way up here in the dark. Besides, there's the coral bead. I think my aunt was killed in the barn, Rob; then somebody brought her body out here to make it look like she'd fallen into that ravine."

"Ginger, this happened an awfully long time ago," Rob said.

"Meaning what? You don't think I should pursue it? Just what am I supposed to do?"

"I know. It's just that I have — well, kind of a funny feeling about this. Frankly, it scares me. I don't want you to get hurt."

We were approaching the small clearing where we'd left the horses and he turned, hands out, to help me over the last stone hurdle. "A likely story," I said. "If there really had been a horse named Beelzebub, you'd have gotten me in the saddle one way or another just so you could see how far he'd throw me!" I started to laugh, but the look on his face stopped me. "Okay, okay! So maybe you do care a little," I said.

"More than a little, Ginger." Rob lifted me over the rock, but he didn't let go. I didn't want him to. I wanted him to kiss me, and he did.

When I was about twelve I had asked my mother how she knew when she fell in love with my father. "Did you hear bells ring when he kissed you?" I asked.

"Better than that," my mother said. "I heard the ocean roar."

When Rob Quillian kissed me, not only did I hear the ocean roar, but I thought I was going to drown in it. I stepped back for breath, took one look at those eloquent gray eyes in that long, bony face, and kissed him again. Thoroughly. "Oh, Lord!" I said. "Let's go home."

"Let's don't." He kissed my ear, then worked around it to my chin.

This wasn't supposed to be happening. "It's getting late," I said. "We promised Ethelene, remember?"

"Ethelene who?"

"Come on, Rob, I mean it." I eased away from him — reluctantly — and untied Sally Gray, hoping I had strength enough to climb into the saddle. I felt like one of those silly, stereotyped characters from a third-rate romance novel. Adverbs I had never used in my life whirled around in my head.

Was this love? I didn't know. I had wanted to fall in love sometime, and there were a few times when I thought I had, but it had never been like this. And with Rob Quillian — funny, comfortable Rob who earned his room and board by the labor of his hands. Well, there was nothing wrong with that! Didn't I do the same thing? But my position here was temporary. . . .

I frowned. Except for elaborating about that ugly dog, Rob seldom talked about his life before coming to Plumb-Nelly. He was a skilled musician, and was obviously well educated. So what was he doing here? Did he have no ambition at all?

The closer we came to the stable, the more my frustration grew. This was the wrong place, the wrong time, and certainly the wrong person. I didn't want to feel this way.

"What's wrong?" Rob asked as we drove the short distance to the tavern. "You haven't said a word since you got in the car."

"Just thinking," I said, glancing at his angular profile. Why did he have to have such a nice face? "I really don't know very much about you. When are you going to fill me in?"

"Well, I've never been infirm, insane, or incarcerated." He leered at me. "Although I could be inspired to be indiscreet under the right circumstances."

I laughed. "Don't forget infuriating! You know what I meant."

He shrugged. "As far as I know, most of my folks wear shoes, know their alphabet, and bay at the moon only on alternate Thursdays."

"Thanks," I said. I wasn't smiling, and made sure he was aware of it. "It was a nice ride." I got out of the car as soon as it came to a stop and started inside. Lucy, enveloped in a huge apron, waved to me from the back steps, where she polished the brass candlesticks that usually sat on the big walnut buffet. She held one up for inspection and whispered, "I don't think Ethelene wants me in her kitchen."

I spoke to her and smiled — or tried to

197

— as I hurried up the steps while Rob loped after me across the lawn. "Ginger, wait —" I heard the car keys jingle in his hands, heard his footsteps on the walk below, but I didn't stop. A shower. That was what I needed. A shower. Or better still, a long, relaxing bath.

But Ethelene had other ideas. "Where've you been? I thought you'd never get back! Reckon you could debone those chickens for the pot pie? I think they're cool enough to handle. I'm fixing to roll out the pastry now."

So much for the long soaking, I thought. "Just give me a minute to change into a skirt!" I called, trying to reach the stairs before Rob. "Be right down." Maybe Rob would give up and go away. I wasn't ready to deal with him right now, and if he had any sense at all, he'd know it.

But he was waiting in the front hall a few minutes later when I came downstairs. "Look, Ginger," he began, then broke off when the phone rang at the front desk. Rob waved a hand at me. "Don't go anywhere . . ."

"Sorry, the chickens await," I said, moving past him through the empty front parlor. I wasn't looking forward to this. If there was anything I hated, it was handling cold, greasy chickens. And there they were —

two congealing carcasses — waiting for the ultimate indignity. I tied an apron around me, pulled on rubber gloves, and attacked. For a few minutes the two of us worked in silence. Ethelene, up to her wrists in flour, thumped the pastry into a pliable oblong and clamped it into a pan, then started on another. I felt rather than heard the swinging door open behind me, and when no one spoke, turned to see Rob standing at the end of the table, his hands gripping the back of a chair.

Ethelene barely glanced at him. "If it's cookies you're wanting, you're out of luck," she said. "You done ate the last of them after lunch."

But Rob finally found his voice, although I had to strain to hear him. "That was the hospital that called just then," he told us, coming to stand beside the housekeeper. "Sheri died half an hour ago."

Chapter Eighteen

"I sure do thank you for helping me out in the dining room tonight," the girl said. "I reckon I'll get the hang of it after a while, but seems like you gotta have about ten pairs of hands and feet to handle that bunch in there."

Her name was Anita and she was large and placid. She wore her brown hair pulled back with a piece of frazzled pink yarn and acted as though the devil himself were breathing down her neck. Maybe he was. I wouldn't feel comfortable taking Sheri Griffin's place at Plumb-Nelly either, especially since the police didn't seem to be one bit closer to finding the person who killed her.

"That's okay, it took me a while too." I smiled back at her as we stacked the last of the soiled dishes on a tray. Unlike her predecessor, Anita had a pleasant disposition, but I wished she weren't so timid. And so boring! I missed Sheri, and was filled with a mixture of sorrow and fear when I thought she might have died in my place.

"Maybe Ethelene will be able to find somebody to help you out before too long," I said. "With Delaney and me both gone all day during the week, it's too much work for the two of you."

Anita scooped up a handful of silverware. "Well, I won't miss her, that's for sure! You're nice to me and all, but Delaney always makes me feel stupid or something. I guess she just doesn't like me."

"Don't worry about it," I told her. "I don't think she likes anybody right now." Including herself, I thought. Delaney was either worried or embarrassed about her involvement with the man who called himself Al Cline. I knew the police had questioned her about the caller's voice when Gideon had telephoned me at the tavern. Could she not recognize the man she knew as "Al" as the person who had called asking for Ginger? But he had either disguised his voice, Delaney said, or it wasn't the same man. And I could almost believe her. Gideon was a talented mimic, and would entertain with impersonations at the least encouragement.

Delaney hadn't brought up the subject of Gideon Foster again, although I was sure she didn't believe he had killed Sheri. If only she knew how much I wanted her to be right! It had been a week since they had heard the girl moaning beneath the bridge in Fiddler's

Meadow, and investigators still didn't seem to be much closer to finding him. The car that had hit Sheri Griffin was discovered in a parking lot in Wilkesboro a few days after she died, but it had been stolen and was obviously hot-wired. Police found no fingerprints other than the ones that belonged there. And if Ethelene's sources were correct, Sheri had planned to meet someone earlier — before her date with the philandering Leonard. According to Sheri's girlfriend Glenda, she had dressed for her date at Glenda's house but left about half an hour early. "Said she had to see somebody," Glenda said. "To talk, she said." But Glenda didn't know who she was meeting or why, only that Sheri hadn't seemed afraid.

Had Sheri Griffin planned to blackmail someone?

Someone matching Gideon's description had stayed in a motel on the outskirts of Morganton for several days before Sheri was killed, but if investigators knew where he went from there, they weren't saying.

I glanced into the front parlor, where Eugenia was rounding up a group for bridge. Rob had disappeared somewhere after dinner, and I didn't want to come face-to-face with him if I could help it. In the sadness and confusion following Sheri's death, my frustration with Rob seemed trivial, and any serious conversation we might have had was put aside. Now I found myself avoiding him, and once during dinner tonight I had noticed him looking at me from across the room with a funny little smile on his face.

"So here you are." A masculine hand closed on my shoulder, and I resisted an impulse to jump. It was Bailey. "I know it's been a long day," he said, "but could I coerce you into singing — even for a little while? I think it would help to put all of us at ease." He took both of my hands in his. "What's that they say about music having charms?"

I tried not to grit my teeth. Music meant Rob. I would have to hear his voice, look into his face — if only I could avoid his eyes! Rob Quillian could express himself more eloquently with his eyes alone than the most impassioned speaker.

I followed Bailey into the front parlor, where Rob flashed his victorious little "gotcha" smile from his seat at the piano. He ran long fingers down the keyboard, winked at me, and said, "Your thoughts for a penny, my elusive Miss Virginny?"

I laughed of course — along with everyone else, but I wished myself anywhere but here. "What would you like to hear?" I asked the group at the card table. Eugenia had succeeded in snaring both the Whitworths and was looking around for a fourth. Bailey, who didn't move fast enough, ended up across from her. "Something slow and soothing," he said. "You know how fierce Eugenia gets at bridge."

Rob dug out a collection of music, and we sang a few Beatles songs that seemed to please our audience. Bailey's uncle Chamblee and several other dinner guests wandered in from the dining room to listen, and even the four card players kept their arguments to a minimum.

When Rob paused to thumb through the pile of sheet music, I was tempted to make excuses and go upstairs early, but he put out a hand to stop me. The sensation of his fingers on mine, if only for a few seconds, brought my feelings rushing to the surface again, and I felt as if I were back in the ninth grade when the cute boy across from me had asked me to the freshman dance in front of the whole class. I looked around. Had anyone noticed my self-consciousness?

"Look at this, Ginger," Rob persisted. "This one's been around awhile!" He propped the music above the keyboard and played a few bars with an exaggerated rolling jangle. "What fun! Sounds like background music for a melodrama."

"My goodness, I haven't heard that in a while!" Kirby Whitworth said. "And it's not from a melodrama. That's from a Broadway musical — *Rose Marie*. They made a movie out of it too."

"With Jeanette MacDonald and Nelson Eddy." Chamblee looked at his sister. "Remember? You thought he was so good-looking."

Lucy nodded, smiling. "They sang 'Indian Love Call.' I thought it was the most romantic thing I'd ever heard!"

"That's in here too." Rob turned the yellowed pages carefully, then looked up at me. "Want to give it a try?"

"Are you kidding? That's about an octave out of my range. Why don't you just play it?"

When he finished, Eugenia put down her cards and sighed. "I'd forgotten about that song. . . . I saw the play, you know. A small theater group came to Asheville while we were on vacation there." She laughed. "It was the first live musical I'd ever seen; didn't think I'd ever forget it!

"Wait a minute!" The fragile cup of sassafras tea tottered as Eugenia shoved back her chair. She stood suddenly and walked over to stare at the painting of the girl in the swing. "*That's* where I saw her! She was in that show."

I glanced at Rob. "Who? Dahlia Brown?"

"I'm sure that's who it was! She wore a dark wig, of course — played an Indian maiden, but there was a reception after the show so we could meet the cast, and she'd changed into street clothes. I remember being surprised at that red hair." Eugenia reached out as if to touch the painting, then changed her mind. "I'd never met an actress before, and she was so beautiful. And young — she didn't look much older than I was, and I couldn't have been more than thirteen or fourteen at the time. And she even gave me her picture. I kept it for a long time."

"Oh, come on, Eugenia!" Lucy Whitworth said. "How can you be sure it's the same woman? After all, this was more than a few years back."

"Well, maybe you're right, but there's definitely a resemblance . . . and I'm still not saying she wasn't." Eugenia looked at me, then glanced quickly away, and I knew: She suspected the reason for my curiosity about the woman who had called herself Dahlia Brown.

"Enough of this! Lighten up, people." Bailey crossed the room and held out his hands to me. "Come on, Ginger . . . how about a dance? Rob, give us some music."

I felt myself being whirled away as Rob

played something innocuous on the piano. Bailey had been more attentive than usual the last few days, and I wondered if he suspected there might be something between Rob and me.

"What about 'Stardust'?" Bailey said to Rob as we waltzed by the piano. "And don't pretend you don't know it!" His hand tightened on my waist as we moved into the empty dining room and swirled down the hall. Bailey Davenport was a very good dancer, and I was beginning to enjoy the impromptu dance, until I realized his intentions. When we reached the door to the parlor, Bailey bent and kissed me quickly on the lips just as the song came to an end, then thanked me for the dance and resumed his card game.

I glanced at Rob, who shuffled the music into an untidy stack and closed the piano — all without looking at me. If Bailey had meant to make Rob Quillian jealous, he seemed to have succeeded.

"Well, if everyone is through with me for the night, I believe I'll go upstairs," I said to Bailey's back. I disliked being used, and wondered if he had the sensitivity to understand my comment.

He did. "Ouch!" Bailey made a face at me as he pulled a make-believe dagger out of his back. "Look, Ginger, I didn't mean —"

He started to get up, but I waved him back into his seat. "It's okay," I said. "I'm just tired; it's been a long day. Good night, everybody." Just before I turned to go upstairs, I noticed Rob was smiling, and that irritated me even more. Were the two of them keeping score?

As I had anticipated, Mrs. T.S.S. lay in wait for me the next morning when I came down for breakfast. "We need to talk," she said, curling a claw around my arm.

I helped myself to cereal and joined her at her table, hoping she wouldn't give me away. "Surely you're aware that there's more than a passing resemblance between you and the girl in that painting," she said. And when I didn't answer right away, Eugenia sighed. "I'm not sure why you're here, Virginia, but I suspect it has something to do with that young woman's death. Am I right?"

I nodded. "I hope you won't say anything about this. I'd rather no one else knew about it just yet."

"Oh, for heaven's sake! Do you take me for a fool? Of course I won't say anything! But if I can figure it out, how many others have come to the same conclusion? These people aren't stupid . . . and aside from the resemblance, you ask entirely too many questions." Eugenia took her time buttering a cranberry muffin. "That thing with your brakes was no accident, and I have a very strong feeling that Sheri saw who did it. I'd be most upset, Virginia Cameron, if that happened to you."

My corn flakes didn't look so appealing anymore. "Please, Eugenia! I'm trying to eat. This is no way to begin a working day. Besides, I don't want to think about it."

She fingered her heavy, gold locket. "Well, you'd better think about it. After all, this woman died . . . what . . . over fifty years ago. What does it matter now?"

"You don't understand," I began. "Dahlia Brown didn't die the way they said. I know because —"

"Look, I don't care if the woman choked to death on a cold biscuit, but I do care about you, Virginia." Eugenia jabbed a finger at me. "And as much as I hate to say it, I think you should leave this place. Go home!"

Home to what? I didn't even know where home was anymore. I needed to think. And to do that I had to be by myself in a place where no one wanted me to sing, dance, or wait on tables. Since I wasn't due at the newspaper for another hour, I changed into walking shoes and followed the path to the cemetery. What better place to be alone? Besides, if Dahlia Brown were here, maybe the mysterious Mason was buried here as well. There was a possibility I had overlooked his grave before.

My feet were wet from dew by the time I had inspected all the stones in the Davenport family plot. No Masons here. A cool wind sent dry leaves scuttering, and overhead a yellow-tinged muscadine vine swayed back and forth in the sweet gum tree. I wondered when they would finally move my aunt's grave. Soon, I hoped. Apart from the rest, it looked as if she had been banished, as if she had done something shameful and didn't deserve to rest with the others.

I stood at her grave and listened as a jet zoomed overhead. My aunt had never seen a jet; she'd never seen television. Her only shame was in dying, and her only hope was in me. I knew Eugenia was right; I should get out — and soon. But I just couldn't leave her now.

Chapter Nineteen

From the top of the hill I saw Delaney's car race down the long drive and disappear in a puff of dust. She had converted the back room of her small store into a workshop for a wandering potter, and for the last few days had thrown herself almost completely into the craft, arriving home late — clay-smeared and weary. I hoped it would last.

It was peaceful here in the old cemetery, and beautiful; I was in no hurry to leave, but work had piled up at *The Bugle* during my absence the week before, and I had a lot of catching up to do. Someone had left a bunch of flowers, now withered and brown, on my aunt's grave. I tossed them out and dumped the yellowed water, then started back to the house with the jar, which, according to the remnant of label, had once held pickles. I smiled, wondering who had put them there. Lucy probably; it seemed like something she would do.

Footsteps on the gravel path below warned me that some one was coming, and I looked around for an alternate route, but it was too late. He had seen me. Bailey Davenport looked up and waved.

Oh, go away! I thought. I don't need any more complications in my life right now. But what could I do? Wave back, of course — and smile. And so I did — at the same time taking long, quick strides to meet him with what I hoped was a determined look on my face.

"Hey, what's the rush? Don't go!" He caught my hand and held it.

"Bailey, I'm late already." I looked at my watch. "Didn't realize the time. Your uncle Chamblee will skin me!"

"Spare me a few minutes, okay?" He flashed his charming Davenport smile at me. "I promise to write an excuse."

I sighed. "I have an appointment at ten with a real live paying customer, but I guess I can give you five minutes." I let him lead me back to the top of the slope, where a gnarled oak stood guard over a tall, stained monument.

Bailey dusted leaves from the low marble wall and offered me a seat. "I'm afraid I haven't been going about this right, Ginger," he said. "I wish I were better at this kind of thing."

"What kind of thing?"

Bailey stared at a point on the horizon

as if he expected something to materialize there, and I'll swear he blushed. "Well, letting you know how I feel." He stood and addressed a bare rosebush in the corner of the lot. "I didn't mean to upset you last night — really."

"What did you mean to do?" I asked. I could enjoy this if I didn't suspect where it was leading.

He turned and looked at me. "I thought we . . . that is, you and I . . ." Bailey shrugged. "Oh, damn! I thought we had something there — but now —"

I didn't know what to say. Bailey Davenport and I had gone out only a few times, kissed once or twice on the stairs. Now and then he showed an interest, I thought; but most of the time he ignored me. I reminded him of this.

He shook his head and sat beside me on the cold stone wall. "You're right . . . I know you're right, but Ginger, I didn't mean for it to seem that way. Oh, hell! Why can't I ever say what I'm thinking?"

I waited. Is this where I was supposed to say, "Oh, Bailey, I didn't know you cared." I reached for his hand. "I've been here only a few weeks. That isn't very long, not long enough."

"It's long enough for me . . ." He gripped

my hand tightly. "Apparently it's long enough for Rob as well."

I drew my hand away. My fingers were red where he had pressed them. "What about Rob?"

"I've seen how he looks at you — seen the two of you together —"

I stood abruptly and started back toward the tavern. "Excuse me, but this is where I came in!" Was the man turning into another Gideon Foster?

"No, wait! I'm sorry." Bailey hurried after me and touched my shoulder. "Look, Ginger, give me a break, will you? I told you I'm new at this! Just promise me you'll think about it; that's all I ask."

I frowned. "Think about what?"

With a hand on my elbow, Bailey turned me to face him. Over his shoulder I could see the graveyard on the hill. "Me. Plumb-Nelly. All of this. I offer you the bones of my ancestors, Virginia Cameron."

Was this a proposal? I started to smile and then realized he was perfectly serious. Before I could speak he scooped me into his arms and kissed me. "I'll be waiting," he reminded me, then walked away, leaving me standing on the hillside breathless and thoroughly perplexed. I was on my way to work before it occurred to me that he hadn't mentioned love.

Eugenia stood at the top of the stairs with the cat in her arms when I went up to change shoes, and I knew she had been waiting for me — probably by the window, and that she knew where I had been. "Is anything wrong?" she asked, giving me a closer look.

I thought about telling her of Bailey's strange proposal, but decided against it. Sometimes I thought she had a little video camera behind those snappy black eyes. I wouldn't be surprised if Eugenia had guessed how Bailey Davenport felt. "I'm fine," I told her. "Just needed to clear my head." I walked with her to the door of her room. "I'll be all right, don't worry."

She stroked the cat. "You're staying, aren't you?"

I nodded. "I have to; for a while, at least."

"I hope you know what you're doing." The door closed softly behind her.

I hope so too, I said to myself. I wish I felt as bold as I sounded. I found myself wanting to follow Eugenia into the security of her large, sunny room, to spend the day in her comfortable rocking chair with Agnes at my feet. No one would dare to bother me there.

I was glad Eugenia was on my side, and I knew I could count on Ethelene Cleveland as well. And Rob. I had always felt at ease around Rob; if only I knew more about him! And from time to time that day, when I began to question my decision to stay, I reminded myself I wasn't alone at Plumb-Nelly Tavern. Had Dahlia Brown done the same?

But my aunt had kept her whereabouts — even her identity — a secret. My family knew where I was. Besides, I told myself, Gideon Foster was running for his life. He wouldn't have the nerve to show his face around Fiddler's Glen, or around me, again. Would he?

It was late when I finally got through at *The Bugle* that afternoon, and I had sent word by Delaney, who dropped by earlier to place an ad, that I would not be back for dinner. One of our new accounts, a large fabric shop in a small community about twenty miles distant, had asked me to pick up some corrected copy, so I knew it would be well past dark before I got to Plumb-Nelly.

The woman who owned the shop was young and energetic, and we discovered while talking that a distant cousin of hers had been my college roommate, so I spent more time there than I had intended. As I started home, my growling stomach reminded me it was past time to eat, and I remembered the diner that

Chamblee had told me about. "Best hot dogs around here, and chili that would singe the pinfeathers off a chicken!"

Somehow the chili didn't appeal to me that much, but I hadn't had a good hot dog in ages, so I turned off at the green neon sign and found a space beside one of the eighteen-wheelers in the parking lot. The restaurant was small and narrow, but looked clean and smelled heavenly, so I slid into an empty booth in the back and gave my order. The customers, mostly truckers, and a few denim-clad locals, seemed to be enjoying the food as well as the camaraderie, and I found myself listening shamelessly to some of their stories. These were big, rugged men who laughed loud and talked rough. But they took off their hats when they entered, held the door for women, and called the elderly waitress "ma'am." Just let anyone try to harm me here!

And my hot dog was good, so good I ordered another, as well as a slab of hot cherry pie with ice cream on top and a free refill on the coffee. The coffee was good too, but I tried to drink the second cup too fast and dribbled some down the front of my gold silk blouse. By the time I had washed it off in the ladies' room and waited for change from my bill, my burly security guards had left.

I looked at my watch as I walked outside. It was almost nine o'clock, and except for a few cars parked around by the side of the building, mine was alone on the lot. For once I did what my mother had always told me to do and looked on the floorboard of the car before getting behind the wheel. I had an uneasy feeling that someone was watching me and hurriedly locked the doors once I was inside. The temperature had dropped, and I pulled my coat closer around me, wishing I had worn gloves. When I finally managed to dig the keys from the bottom of my pocketbook, it seemed to take me forever to find the right one with my cold, stiff fingers.

I looked behind me after I had driven a few miles, but saw nothing. The road seemed deserted; still, the uneasiness persisted, and I accelerated in my eagerness to get home. I had driven this route before and knew I was within five miles of the familiar entrance to Plumb-Nelly. In a few minutes I would be there.

The narrow road stretched in front of me, then curved left through Fiddler's Meadow and the bridge where Sheri, wearing my cape, had waited for death. And there on the asphalt just past the bridge, a human body — or what looked like a human body — lay directly in the path of my car!

Brakes squealed like an animal screaming as I came to a stop inches in front of the shape and stepped out of the car. Whatever it was, it didn't move, and when I looked closer I saw why. Someone had filled a large burlap bag with grass clippings, and used a pumpkin for a head to create this crude likeness of a person. Someone had meant me to stop.

The pumpkin rolled to one side as I gave the lumpy form an angry kick, scattering the stuffing. Then, as I turned to get back into the car, I heard the pounding of horse's hooves on the hard-packed ground. The dark rider appeared from behind the old church on my right, bolted across the road a few yards in front of me, and galloped over the meadow.

I think I was so startled that for a minute I forgot to be frightened. But when the strains of fiddle music came from the horseman in the distance, I remembered what my feet were for. Thank goodness the car started up right away, and I think I squashed the pumpkin in my headlong rush to leave. I would never hear Stephen Foster's music again without reliving that sickening moment. "Jeanie with the Light Brown Hair" wafted back to me from the figure on the horse.

Chapter Twenty

"What did he look like?" Eugenia demanded. "Could you tell what he was wearing?"

"I don't know . . . I couldn't see. Something gray, I think. It was too dark." I sat by the low fire in the parlor and sipped brandy. It tasted a little like varnish smelled and made my eyes water, but if it would make me forget what I'd just seen, I would gladly drain the decanter.

Delaney sprawled on one end of the sofa, nibbling peanuts one by one. "It was probably just Pete Barnwell out for a ride on one of his horses," she said without looking up.

"Funny that he should come along just as I stopped for that dummy in the road," I said.

"What dummy? Are you people talking about me again?" Bailey came in with a load of firewood, and I had to start my story from the beginning.

I could tell from his expression that he didn't take me seriously, but he did drive down to the bridge to see if the dummy was there.

He was back in ten minutes. "I didn't see

any dummy, but it did look like somebody had dropped a pumpkin in the road — splattered all over the place! Probably rolled off the back of a truck." Bailey picked up Agnes and sat on the rug beside my chair. "Are you sure about that dummy, Ginger? I mean, it was dark along there, and after what happened to Sheri —"

"I didn't imagine the figure in the road, and I didn't imagine the man on the horse either." I took a last sip of brandy and looked calmly into the fire. To hell with them! I didn't care if they believed me or not. "Somebody went to a lot of trouble to set me up — even to the appropriate Stephen Foster song."

Bailey frowned. "What do you mean?"

I stood and put my empty glass on the mantel; I really wanted to hurl it into the fire. "I mean I heard somebody playing 'Jeanie with the Light Brown Hair' — on a fiddle," I said.

Delaney smiled. "How can somebody ride and play a fiddle at the same time?"

"Willie Hugh Jordan did it," Bailey said. "The night he came back for his Jean — or at least that's what they say." He shrugged. "But then, he was a ghost."

I felt his hands on my shoulders. "Good Lord, Ginger! You're as tense as a statue!

Here, sit down and let me —"

I moved away from him, pausing at the door. "No thanks, I think I'll just go up and try to get some sleep — that is if you'll all promise not to try to have me committed overnight. There *was* a dummy in the road tonight . . . somebody put it there just for me. And I don't really care how the horseman played the fiddle! All I want to know is why."

Eugenia stood to follow me upstairs. "I think I know how," she said in a voice loud enough to reach even those Davenports on the hill behind us. "Haven't any of you ever heard of a tape player?"

"Thank you," I told her as we walked upstairs together. "It's nice to have at least one friend who doesn't think I'm certifiable." Ethelene had gone home earlier, and I missed Mercer Belle's comfortable chatter. The halls seemed quieter than usual. "Where's Rob?" I asked as we stood in the dim upstairs corridor.

"Took the day off. Said there were things he had to see to. Why?" I don't know many people who glower, but Eugenia did. "Surely you don't think he had anything to do with your galloping ghost out there?"

"Of course not," I said. But I wasn't sure he hadn't. I wasn't sure about anything. "And it wasn't any ghost." I found myself standing by the double doors to the porch staring at the space where a swing once hung. "Somebody's following the same old pattern: I saw the rider, heard Lucifer's fiddle — now what? Am I supposed to end up at the bottom of Devil's Bluff?"

Probably. Eugenia didn't say so, but we both knew I was on somebody's hit list. I would have been glad of even Agnes's company that night, but she had deserted me for Eugenia. The cat's distrust of my room had something to do with the dresser that I was certain had once been my aunt's. And as a matter of fact, I wasn't entirely at ease with the dried-flower smell that emanated from its middle drawer or the vase of daisies that sometimes reflected in its mirror.

Tonight the mirror remained blank except for the likeness of my haggard-looking countenance — complete with circles under my eyes and wild, untamed hair. I lay curled under the patchwork quilt and stared at the dark glass until my eyes ached, listening for Rob's footsteps in the hall. Where was he when I needed him? And who had staged the "ghost rider" for my benefit in Fiddler's Meadow?

"Well, it could've been Bailey Davenport,

I suppose," Eugenia admitted at breakfast. "He went to his room after dinner — or at least that's what he said. Nobody saw him leave, but that's not to say he didn't."

But according to Bailey's aunt, he was terrified of horses. The horseman I had seen was not only skilled but confident. "What about Delaney?" I asked.

"Came in just before you did. Said she'd been to the shop — and she did have clay on her hands. Had to wash before she'd come in the parlor."

How convenient. "Are you sure it was clay?" I asked.

Eugenia laughed. "At my age, I'm not even sure what my name is, but it looked like clay.

"I'm not saying she couldn't have done it," she added. "She had time to get here before you if she cut across that back field . . . but how did she manage to move the dummy out of the road before Bailey got there? He said it was gone, remember?"

I nodded, frowning. "I know that's what he *said*, Eugenia."

For once she was speechless. "Oh," she said, staring back at me. "I didn't think of that."

"Eugenia's worried about you," Rob told me that afternoon when he stopped by *The*

Bugle. "And frankly, so am I. I hear Ichabod Crane paid you a visit in the meadow last night."

"Either Ichabod or his first cousin," I said, trying to disguise my relief at seeing him again. "Only I'm supposed to think it was the soldier ghost — Willie Hugh Jordan on his horse Biscuit. The fiddler."

Rob lowered his voice. "Aren't you the least bit curious about where I went yesterday?"

"Should I be?" I was, of course.

"Did a little checking on my way back from Charlotte. Your great-aunt died from a broken neck."

"How do you know?"

He shrugged. "Matter of public record. I looked it up in the register of deeds at the county courthouse. Unless there's been a fire or something like that, they have files going back before the turn of the century."

"Was there anything else?"

"Kneecap was shattered — right arm too, but a fracture of the cervical spine was listed as cause of death. That's a broken neck in layman's terms, I'm told."

"That could have happened as well if she'd been pushed from the loft," I said.

"There's another thing," Rob added with a glance toward Chamblee's office. "There didn't seem to be many contusions, or if

225

there were, they didn't mention them. How could she have fallen from the top of a rocky cliff without a lot of cuts and bruises . . . unless she was already dead when he put her there?"

The silence seemed to go on forever. "I don't like this," I said. It came out in a rabbity little whisper.

"I know." Rob frowned. "Tell me about this phantom horseman. Where did you first see him?"

"I think he came from that old church across the road. It — he must've been waiting in those trees behind the cemetery."

"That's right, there is an old graveyard back there." Rob leaned across the counter and whispered, "What time can you get away?"

"Five o'clock, I guess, unless something comes up. Why?"

"Meet me there . . . No, better still, I'll come by for you here," Rob said. "It might not be a good idea for you to go out there alone."

It was still light when I followed Rob's dingy gray Plymouth to the small frame church beside Fiddler's Meadow. The building was old and in need of paint, and according to the dates on some of the stones out back, probably sat on the same site as many others before it. A peeling sign out front read LIBERTY CREEK PRESBYTERIAN, named, I assumed, for the stream that ran through the meadow.

"Do you mind telling me what we're looking for?" I asked Rob as I trailed after him among the markers. "Surely you don't expect the horseman to come charging out in broad daylight."

He squatted to inspect a dark-stained slab, then moved on to read another. "I imagine he came from the other side of these woods, which means it could be anybody," he said. "But I'm looking for the fiddler — what was his name? Willie . . . something? The Confederate soldier who was killed."

"Willie Hugh Jordan. The ghost, you mean?" I stooped to run my fingers along a chipped granite stone. "You're right — he would be buried here, wouldn't he? If his relatives knew where he was killed, they'd want him brought home." Was I meant to believe the ghostly rider had come from the grave itself? A mourning dove called from the woods behind us, and something moved in the dry weeds at my feet. A lizard maybe. I hoped it was a lizard.

"Hey! Over here. Here's the Jordan plot!" Rob called to me from a tree-shaded spot near the rear of the building. I saw him kneel beside a small lichen-covered headstone and touch the black carved letters. "Here it is, Ginger. Willie Hugh Jordan. Died in 1863 . . ." Rob brushed off his hands and stood. "He was only twenty-two."

I looked at the stones around me. Was his sweetheart buried here too? Or did she marry someone else? In any case, she would be buried with her own family. I hurried away, swallowing a great big knot in my throat. The place seemed desolate and sad, and I wondered if any of Willie Hugh's relatives still lived in Fiddler's Glen. Willie Hugh Jordan had died in battle, a hero in the eyes of his fellow soldiers and to those he left behind. If I were one of the Jordan kin, I would be mad as the devil to learn that some one had used his dying as a prank.

I started for my car, slipping my arms into the sweater I had thrown around me, but Rob still lagged behind. "Let's go! Ethelene's serving apple pie tonight, and there won't be a piece left!" I felt a little guilty at how my fickle spirits rose at the prospect of the rich dessert, but not too guilty. I looked over my shoulder to find him climbing the hill in the other direction. "What on earth are you doing now?"

He didn't stop. "Looking for Mason. Doesn't look like anybody's been buried here since the 1960s, but if it was a last name, we might find the family."

Groaning, I plodded back up the slope and scanned the other side, but the place seemed Mason-less. "As much as I hate to admit it, you have a point. I was looking for the name in the Davenports' cemetery; it didn't occur to me that Mason might be buried somewhere else."

"And it might not be a *he*." Rob spoke from a corner of the graveyard where faded plastic Easter lilies remained from almost seven months before. "Did you ever consider the possibility that Mason was a woman?"

I looked at him standing against a backdrop of flaming dogwood and could only guess at how beautiful it would be here in the spring. *Plastic* Easter lilies? And for some reason I thought of Grace Millsap. "What was Otto's mother's maiden name?" I asked.

"Duckworth," Ethelene told me when I slipped into the kitchen after dinner. "Daddy was Clayton Duckworth from over near —"

"Then there weren't any Masons in her family?" I asked.

"Good Lord! Why do you want to know that?" Ethelene crammed another bowl into a jam-packed refrigerator. "Nearly everybody around here's got Masons in their family. Why my own daddy belonged — Granddaddy too."

I laughed. "No, I mean a family named Mason. A friend of mine back home thinks she might have relatives from around here."

"Oh." Ethelene scratched her chin. "Well then . . . only one I can think of was old Miss Gertrude Mason. She was a widow woman, but we called her Miss . . . died — Lord, must've been twenty, thirty years ago, but she has a granddaughter somewhere around here."

"Who?" I said. "Where?"

Ethelene carefully folded the dishtowel, watching me all the while. She knew I was lying, but she wasn't going to challenge me. Yet. "Rhonda something or other . . . married a Dixon. No! Her daddy was a Dixon . . . I think her married name is Campbell. Rhonda Campbell. Used to be a cashier at that new supermarket in Lenoir."

I found Rob listening just outside the door in the dining room, where he pretended to run a carpet sweeper under the tables. "I think Ethelene wants more than that two-foot-square area swept," I told him. "If you wanted to listen, why didn't you just come in?"

"Look, it's stretching it to expect her to

swallow that lie about your *friend's* local connections. She might really get suspicious if *I* showed an interest too." And then as if to make up for lost time, he began to sweep in earnest, pausing only to move aside a chair. "I couldn't hear everything she said," Rob admitted. "Are there any Masons around here still?"

I told him about the cashier in Lenoir. "It's not very far. Maybe we could drive over during lunch break tomorrow. And I'll check the files at *The Bugle;* they might have something on the Playhouse cast that summer." I straightened a yellow chrysanthemum in its cut-glass bowl, refolded a couple of napkins. "If this doesn't lead to something, I don't know where else to look. . . ."

The carpet sweeper crashed to the floor with a bang, grabbing my attention as it was meant to do. Rob's expression looked something like Wile E. Coyote's when he sees the shadow of the boulder just before it smashes him, and I looked up in time to see the hall door closing.

Someone had been standing there, listening. I wondered just how much they had heard.

Chapter Twenty-one

"What in the world are you doing under that desk?" I asked Eugenia the next morning as I hurried downstairs. I leaned over the banister to get a better look. This usually stiff-backed woman was crawling around on her hands and knees, poking about with her cane. I knew better than to laugh.

She swore as her rigid, black-clad fanny bumped into a brass planter and sent it rocking, then pulled herself to her feet and glared at me. "Have you seen Agnes?" One strand of her hair had come loose and stuck out like a rooster's tail over her face.

I just stood there, staring back. This couldn't be Eugenia! Maybe I'd better go back upstairs and come down again.

"For heaven's sake! Agnes. The cat!" Eugenia thumped the floor with her cane. "Can't imagine where she's gotten to. I let her out early this morning and haven't seen her since." She peered out the window to the porch, then tossed aside a sofa cushion. "She usually comes when I call."

"Oh, she'll turn up," I said. "You know

how fickle she is." Agnes had probably decided to take up with someone else — someone who had offered her cheese; she loved cheese — but I didn't want to be the one to tell Eugenia, since she'd taken such a fancy to her. I looked at my watch. I had less than fifteen minutes to grab a piece of toast from the kitchen and get to work on time. "I'll ask Ethelene," I said. "Maybe she's seen her."

Eugenia drooped — actually *drooped* — into a chair and clasped her bejeweled hands in front of her. "No. I asked. She hasn't. No one has."

I patted her arm. "Well, don't worry, she probably has a boyfriend somewhere. She'll come back." I didn't have time to worry about Agnes with all the other things going on, although I did feel a pang of guilt at leaving Eugenia sitting there, looking so forlorn. I wondered if it had been Eugenia who eavesdropped at the door the night before, and decided it hadn't. If Mrs. T.S.S. wanted to know what we were saying, she would have walked boldly into the room and listened.

Rob and I were planning to drive to Lenoir in search of Rhonda Campbell as soon as we could get away for lunch. But even if we found her, I didn't have the slightest idea what to ask.

"Kind of like going on a treasure hunt, isn't it?" Rob said as we started out a few hours later. "The Great Supermarket Survey: I can see us now, snooping up and down maze-like aisles, looking for clues in the Hamburger Helper."

I giggled. "Did you ever find out which store it was?"

"Ethelene just said, 'That new one on the right just as you come in.' It's next to a furniture outlet, she thinks."

The "new" supermarket, we discovered, had been there for fourteen years, and Rhonda Campbell had been gone for three. "I think she's still at that garden center over on Briggs Street," the manager said. "Her daddy-in-law started the business a few years ago and she left here to help him out."

We finally tracked down our prey between the wind chimes and the potted chrysanthemums, and I ended up buying one of each, but Rhonda Campbell had no idea who our Mason might have been.

None of the Masons, that Rhonda could recall, had had any connection with either the troupe of actors or the tavern. She didn't even know who the Davenports were. "Maybe it was a stage name," she suggested.

I looked at Rob, who shrugged. "It's possible," he said. Were we grasping at straws?

"Well, so much for Rhonda," Rob said as we drove back to Fiddler's Glen. "But her idea's worth looking into. If Mason was a pseudonym, maybe he . . . or she is listed in the ads. Have you looked in the newspaper files?"

"Haven't had time." It had been a busy morning, I explained. Besides, looking through all those old bound copies was a dirty, backbreaking chore. "If you think all I have to do is twist a little knob and scan microfilm, think again," I told him. "And then everybody wants to know what you're looking for. I'm waiting for Uncle Chamblee to leave, and he's taking this afternoon off."

"Good." Rob glanced at me as he stopped for a light. "Ginger, who knew you'd be coming through Fiddler's Meadow the other night? Somebody had your timing down to the second."

"It could've been almost anybody. Chamblee Davenport recommended the diner; he knew I'd be too late for dinner. Delaney too. I asked her to tell Ethelene I wouldn't be there. And then anybody who dropped by the tavern would know if they asked."

He nodded. "That about covers it, doesn't it?"

I told him about the feeling I'd had when I left the diner, the feeling that someone was watching. "I suppose somebody could have phoned from a car — or even from the diner itself, although I didn't recognize anybody in there."

"Or the person on horseback was watching from that hill across the road. That old churchyard is only a few miles from the diner, and there's a dirt road leading through those woods behind it."

"How do you know?" I asked.

Rob reached for my hand. "I took the time to look, that's how. Yesterday while we were poking around that graveyard I found tracks where somebody on a horse had come through the woods . . . and it looked like they might have waited up there awhile. Ground was pawed, and there's a good view of the road from there." He looked briefly at my palm and kissed it. "Don't worry, you have a long lifeline."

"You don't know how relieved I am to hear that," I said. I didn't ask him about my love line.

It was past quitting time before I could sneak into the little back room where old copies of *The Bugle* accumulated dust, and then I had to claw through spider webs to find the brittle copies from the summer of 1936. The yellowed pages had a scorched smell and crumbled when I turned them, but most of the editions were only eight pages long and there weren't many of them. Aside from a few advertisements announcing the summer production, described as a musical variety show, I found no mention of the actors until a late July issue when a society editor got carried away with an account of a picnic at Plumb-Nelly.

The event was Lucy Davenport's birthday, and guests included Kirby Whitworth (no surprise!), her brother Chamblee, and several people whom I assume were local friends, as well as Dahlia Brown and Hal Templeton, who were visiting actors with Showtime South. Guests participated in a scavenger hunt on horseback, the paper said, with Chamblee's team winning the prize.

I smiled when I read the final sentence. The hostess was assisted in serving by Grace Duckworth.

An issue three weeks later gave a front-page account of Dahlia Brown's death.

The body of Dahlia Brown, about 20, was found early Sunday in a ravine near Devil's Bluff.

William Harris, 17, who discovered

the body while fishing in Liberty Creek, said his dog led him to the young woman, who was lying in a tangle of muscadine vines beneath an outcropping of rock. Investigators believe she became lost and stumbled from the ledge, falling a distance of several hundred feet.

Miss Brown, a member of the actors' group "Showtime South," was staying at Plumb-Nelly Tavern, where the troupe performed this summer.

Local police have asked anyone who has any information about Miss Brown's family or home address to notify them or Joshua Davenport at the tavern.

I seethed as I made copies of the articles in the duplicating machine. Didn't the police wonder why a young woman was wandering alone up there in the dark? Did everybody believe that ridiculous story about the fiddler? And Joshua Davenport. I had seen his gravestone, hadn't I? He must have been Bailey's grandfather.

Rob waited for me on the back porch, and I showed him the articles as we sat on the steps together. "Now. How do we find Hal Templeton?" I asked.

"Good question. If anyone would remember, it would be Lucy, but then we'd have to explain why we wanted to know."

"*We* would," I reminded him. "But Eugenia wouldn't. Remember how she went on about seeing Dahlia Brown in that musical? We could get her to ask about Hal Templeton. After all, if she remembered one, it wouldn't be so strange for her to remember another. Well . . . would it?"

Rob sighed and looked at me. "Would you mind very much if I took you in my arms and made love to you?" he said. "It's been on my mind a lot lately."

Now, why did he have to say that? Couldn't he tell I would like nothing better? I took a deep breath and swallowed my lust. "I think Eugenia suspects who I am," I said. "We might as well tell her the whole story."

He nodded silently. I could tell he was disappointed, but what did he expect? I didn't care if he wasn't listed in Dun & Bradstreet, but I did want him to be listed in something. The phone book would have been a start. "I'll speak to Eugenia at supper," he said.

But Eugenia wasn't in a mood for conversation. Agnes, it seemed, had forsaken her for an interlude of romance, or perhaps for someone who owned a dairy, and our friend only picked at her meal, although she did drink her usual pot of tea. I brought down my flute, and Rob and I entertained the tavern's guests for over an hour after dinner, but Mrs. T.S.S. never put in an appearance.

"Do you think we should check on Eugenia?" I asked Bailey as I started up to bed. "It's not like her to act this way. Maybe something really has happened to Agnes."

But Bailey just smiled. "If only you were as concerned about me! Don't worry, Ginger. Eugenia fairly wallows in dramatics. Let the woman enjoy a good pout."

I had to admit he had a point, but I hesitated in the hall outside her door before going to my room. If she were asleep, I didn't want to wake her, yet I felt something wasn't right.

Dahlia Brown must have felt it too. I woke to see the eerie reflection of daisies in my mirror when I knew none were there. My room was cold and my eyes ached from lack of sleep. If I hadn't been terrified, I would have burrowed under the covers and ignored the whole thing, but ghost flowers are a little hard to dismiss — especially when I knew why they were there. I looked at the clock by my bed and wasn't surprised to learn I had slept only a little over an hour. But then, what did Dahlia Brown care about sleep?

The house was dark and heavy with silence, and I felt as if I were the only living person in it. Except for Rob, I was alone on our hall, and his door was closed. I knocked sharply, but no one answered. It was after midnight; where else could he be? Abandoning all pretense at silence, I opened his door and let it bang against the wall. His bed was empty.

Dahlia Brown stood in the corridor beside Eugenia's door with impatience evident in every inch of her translucent little being. No, not impatience — fear. Her eyes pleaded with me to hurry, and I knew then Eugenia was in trouble.

Her door was unlocked, and when I switched on the light I saw that her bed was slightly rumpled, and there was a shallow indentation in her pillow, but she hadn't even bothered to turn down the covers. A quick look around told me that Eugenia wasn't there, and probably hadn't been there for some time.

The cat. Had she gone looking for Agnes and fallen some where? Where would I go if I were a cat? The barn, of course. The dark barn with its sagging doors and rotting timbers, and with jagged objects lying about. Spiders. And rats. But would fastidious Eugenia Tyler Stafford-Smith wander alone at night to a foul place like that? Even for Agnes? Not now, not ever!

I felt rather than saw my ghostly aunt's

absence, and hurried into the hallway to see her descending the stairs. Looking back, she hesitated before continuing down the dim passage that led to the rear of the house. I fumbled for the flashlight that Bailey kept in the cloakroom and stumbled after her. "I hope you know where you're going," I said, grabbing a coat from a peg in the hall. I didn't know whose it was and didn't care. I had pulled baggy corduroy pants and a sweatshirt over my flannel pajamas and shoved my icy feet into boots, yet I still shivered.

A cold wind blew, and I stood for a moment on the back porch, dreading to venture out in it. My guide had disappeared or dematerialized, or whatever it is that ghosts do when they vanish from sight, and I looked around frantically, when I heard a noise in the fringe of trees to my right. I was ready to follow when it occurred to me that Dahlia Brown never made a sound, and I was almost grateful to see her appear again on the road that led to the barn.

Icy wind whipped into my face, slicing under my turned-up collar as I hurried after the phantom figure with the beautiful sad eyes. I took big, clomping steps, trying — and failing — to avoid frozen ruts, and jumped blindly across gaping ditches. The barn door was closed, and that kind of surprised me because the hinges were loose and it wouldn't hang straight unless it was propped.

The heavy door almost fell on me when I pulled at the dangling handle, and Dahlia moved on inside without even bothering to look back. I shoved the splintered wood aside and followed her, wishing I had never left Shell City, Florida. Maybe she didn't care if I lay smashed as flat as a paper doll in the weed-choked barnyard. Maybe she wanted company in the hereafter — or wherever she was. Immediate company.

"Hey!" I called after her. "Wait a minute, will you? I can't see a thing in here!" I stood in the gaping doorway and looked around. *Now* where did she go?

And then I saw her standing by the door to the room full of junk, the tiny back room where Rob and I had found the old porch swing, and for the first time I noticed the smell: the smell of hot, melting tallow. I sniffed. Someone was burning a candle!

Chapter Twenty-two

The door was blocked by three large bales of pine straw and a heavy sack of grass seed, and Dahlia Brown was no help at all in shoving them aside. I yelled and pushed and pulled and kicked, and then yelled some more until I had the doorway clear, but nobody came to give me a hand. I didn't really expect anyone.

Eugenia lay on her side with her arms stretched over her head, and I thought she was dead until I heard her moan. The candle, a stub about two inches long, sat in a metal holder in a mound of straw a few feet away, and in another couple of minutes it would ignite the whole thing — barn and all.

I pinched out the flame with my fingers and turned the light on Eugenia's face. She grimaced and tried to sit up. Her glasses slid halfway down her long nose. "What happened?" I asked. "Are you hurt?"

Eugenia whimpered and gripped her head as if she were trying to hold it in place. "Green raincoat," she said.

I put an arm around her and tried not to

think about rats. "What about a green raincoat?" The gold locket, I noticed, still hung around her neck.

Her head bobbed to one side, and she yawned. "Green raincoat."

How was I going to get her out of there? Eugenia wasn't large, but she was a little taller than I was, and I was afraid to leave her while I went for help. My friendly ghost, I noticed, had taken a powder, and having done her duty was probably relaxing in some cozy, dry, well-lighted spirit nook drinking warm milk — evaporated, of course. All I could think to do was scream.

I had opened my mouth to bellow when I heard the crunch of footsteps outside and Rob's wonderful, beautiful voice calling my name.

"Ginger! I thought that was you. My God, what's going on out here?" I felt so warm and snug in those few seconds in his arms, I was almost willing to dismiss poor Eugenia and leave her lying there — at least for a few minutes longer, but my conscience wouldn't let me.

"I found her here," I said. "I think she's drugged; we've got to get her out." I showed him the candle in its nest of straw. "Somebody meant to have a bonfire . . . make that a *barn* fire!"

Eugenia looked up at us and made a face. "Ugh . . . get me out of here!"

"We will." Rob held her face in his hands. "Eugenia, does it hurt to move? Did anyone hit you? Who did this?"

"Don't know . . . just sleepy. Cold." She shivered as Rob put his jacket around her.

"Maybe somebody gave her an injection," I said. "She mentioned a green raincoat. We need to get her to a doctor. Now."

"Let me know if I'm hurting you," Rob said as he carefully lifted her from the floor. "I'm going to take you outside." He kicked at one of the bales of pine straw as we edged through the doorway and I told him how they had blocked the entrance. "If she came to, she wouldn't have been able to get out. And when the barn burned, no one would have known they were there," I said. "The evidence would go up with the building." And Eugenia, I added silently.

"Eugenia, do you remember how you got out here?" Rob asked his nodding burden, but she only grunted.

I looked at Eugenia's feet. The bottoms of her shoes were clean. "She didn't walk, that's for sure!" I sidestepped a frozen puddle. "Somebody put her there. Probably meant for it to look like she'd gone looking for the cat." I patted the pocket of the coat I wore to make sure the candle and its holder were where I had put them. Maybe the would-be murderer had left prints.

"That cat! We should ask Ethelene to make her a cheese souffle." Rob puffed as he stepped over a rut. "If she hadn't waked me, I wouldn't have been outside — wouldn't have heard you yelling."

"Where were you? I looked for you, but you were gone."

He paused to shift his armload gently. Eugenia had gone limp, and her pulse was slow, but steady, thank goodness. "Agnes came crying to my door," Rob said. "Woke me up — and I knew Eugenia had been worried about her, so I got up to let her in." He groaned. "But Agnes didn't want to be in my room, she wanted to be in Eugenia's. I followed her, and she stood out there by her door, carrying on something awful! I was afraid she'd wake the household, so I opened Eugenia's door to let her in. . . ."

"And Eugenia was gone," I said. "I know. But where did you go? You weren't in your room when I looked."

"Damn cat led me all over the place! When Agnes saw that Eugenia wasn't there, she streaked downstairs and squirmed out through a window in the sun room, which is how she probably got inside in the first place, so I followed her, hoping she'd lead me to Eugenia. I thought she'd gone outside to look for the cat and had hurt herself somehow. For all I knew, she was lying out here in the dark somewhere."

"Well, you weren't wrong there," I said, hurrying up the back steps to open the door. "That must have been you I heard when I was on the porch . . . over in those trees on the other side of the house."

"I was making a circle — didn't think Eugenia would go very far in the dark. I was just getting ready to wake Bailey when I heard you shouting."

"Wake Bailey for what? What's going on out here?" Bailey Davenport stumbled out of his doorway into the hall. He wore a faded red bathrobe and ran a hand over his dark, unruly hair. "I thought I heard somebody yelling a while ago. Ginger — what's wrong? What happened to Eugenia?"

I told him, or tried to, while we put Mrs. T.S.S. to bed with a heating pad and heaped the covers on her. She couldn't get warm, she said. And at Eugenia's mumbled request I removed her locket and put it on the table beside her bed, noticing the engraving in ornate script: *A.T.M.* "Her grandmother's," Bailey said. "I've never seen her without it."

While we waited for Sam Molloy I sat by her bed and told the others how I had awakened to discover Eugenia missing, then found her almost unconscious in the barn. "Another few minutes and it might have been too late," I said. "That old place would have gone up like kindling."

Bailey frowned at me. "How did you know where to look?"

I glanced quickly at Rob, who gave me a knowing smile. "Well, I just put myself in Agnes's place. If I were a cat, I'd be on the prowl for mice out there, and I considered the chance — the slim chance, mind you — that Eugenia might have gone there looking for her. But Eugenia didn't get there on her own. Somebody put her there."

"What makes you think that? She might have put that candle there herself." Delaney, whose room was next door, had been awakened by all the commotion and now stood at the window, watching for Sam Molloy.

I told them about the obstructions by the door and how the candle was nestled in straw. "I think somebody shut Agnes out there earlier," I said. "They probably meant for her to die too, but she ran out when they opened the door to unload Eugenia."

"Thank goodness!" Rob squeezed Eugenia's hand. "Somebody wants our Mrs. T.S.S. out of the way. But why?"

I was glad to hear tires on the drive below. I had an idea why somebody might want Eugenia dead, but this wasn't the time to express it.

"I can't find any needle marks or any signs of blows to the head," Sam said after examining Eugenia. "Does anyone know what she had to eat tonight?"

"Not much of anything," I said. "She said she wasn't hungry."

"What about medications? Does she take anything?"

"Eugenia's amazingly healthy for someone her age," Bailey said. "I don't think she has any major problems. You'd know it, Sam, if she did, but I'll look in her medicine cabinet just to be sure."

"I'll go with you," Rob said. "Don't want to miss anything." He made it sound innocent, but I knew he was being a watchdog, and I was glad. They returned with a half-filled bottle of vitamin C, a small tin of aspirin, a vial of over-the-counter eye drops, and an ancient jar of mentholated chest rub.

Sam waved them aside. "We'll have somebody take a look at these, but I don't think there's anything there." He looked at Bailey. "Was she unusually lethargic? Slur her speech?"

"I don't think so. I didn't notice . . . Delaney?"

"She ate alone," his sister said. "But she does that a lot. The last time I saw her, she was drinking that tea. Then I guess she went up to bed."

Sam Molloy put his bag on the floor and stood. "What tea? Would any still be around?"

"She drinks this sassafras concoction," I told him as we went through the kitchen trash. "I don't know where she gets it, but it comes in bags — big enough to brew a pot at a time. Ethelene keeps them in a canister in the pantry."

Ethelene had thrown out the remaining tea and washed the pot, but I knew the tea bag had been discarded in the garbage, which, tied neatly in a plastic bag, waited to be taken to the Dumpster. Going through its contents was not a bit fun.

"Here's where she keeps it," Rob said, holding up the tin. "There are still a few bags in here."

"And this must be the one she used." I dug out a moist, limp square with bits of eggshell sticking to it and sniffed. It had a sweet root-beer smell.

"Let me see that." Sam deposited the tea bag in a saucer and took it over to the light by the kitchen sink, where he poked it gently with one finger. "I don't want to handle this thing too much, but look — you can see a piece of thread sticking out . . . there. Looks as if somebody cut a slit in the bag and then tried to sew it up again. See, there's still a little gap there."

I held out a plastic freezer bag. "This should do to keep it until the police come."

Bailey frowned. "The police?"

"I called them a few minutes ago," Rob said. "Somebody deliberately drugged Eugenia tonight, and they weren't planning to stop there."

"Sheri's death was no accident either," I told him. Not to mention what happened to my brakes, I thought.

"My God! You don't think Al — Gideon — whatever his name is —"

"I don't know," I said. But I lied. I didn't think Gideon Foster had anything to do with what was going on at Plumb-Nelly Tavern.

And it seemed as if I was right. When Ron Slater arrived with another officer a few minutes later, the young police man took me aside. "Looks like they've finally located this Foster guy," he told me. "Thought you'd want to know."

I nodded gratefully. "Gideon? Where?"

"Somewhere up near Canada. Must've been

trying to get as far away as he could."

"He didn't deny calling me, did he? Being here?"

"No, but he swears he wasn't around when Sheri was killed. Says he left that same night after you made it clear you didn't want to see him."

"I wish I could be sure of that," I said.

"Night clerk at a motel up in Virginia backs him up," Rob said. "Checked in at a little before ten, he says. There's no way he could've made that kind of time if he'd killed Sheri."

I felt like kissing the man. I found myself crying instead.

"Hey, look — this loser won't bother you anymore." The policeman gave me an awkward pat on the shoulder. "He knows we'll be watching him now . . . I think this girl's murder about scared him half to death. And of course we'll check out his story; you can be sure of that! But I think you've heard the last of Gideon Foster."

There was no way he could have known I was crying from relief, but I thanked him anyway. I think I thanked him about three times. I was so busy being grateful that I wasn't responsible for Sheri's death that I almost forgot to give him the candlestick I had left in the pocket of my borrowed coat.

If only I could remember where I'd put it.

Chapter Twenty-three

I found the coat where I had left it — folded over the back of a chair in Eugenia's room, and breathed a little easier when I felt the candlestick in the pocket. Even though I had tried to be careful, I knew my fingerprints would be on it, but maybe they wouldn't be the only ones.

Rob and I took time about sitting with Eugenia, who slept until a little after noon the next day. Except for some grogginess and an extreme aversion to sassafras tea, she seemed to suffer no ill effects.

Sam Molloy called to say the lab had found traces of a drug contained in sleeping pills in the residue in her used tea bag. The person who had put it there had simply inserted the tablets through a small incision in the bag, then stitched it up again. The remaining bags had not been tampered with. "Thank goodness it was only enough to put her under for a while but not enough to kill her," he said.

With my help, Eugenia had gone through the rituals of bathing, dressing, and makeup

— including a manicure, and now she sat propped by pillows in a chair by the window while I plied her with Ethelene's rich chicken soup.

"Tell me about the green raincoat," I said, offering her a rice-filled spoonful.

She chewed thoughtfully and washed it down with hot cider. "That's it; that's all I remember. I came upstairs last night too sleepy even to put on my nightgown, and the next thing I knew somebody was carrying me outside." Eugenia shivered and pulled her lap robe a little higher. "It was cold, and windy — too dark to see, but I remember looking down at his coat. It was green — kind of a forest green. I got another glimpse of it when I was left in the barn — when he lit the candle, I guess. I was too drowsy to notice much."

"You keep saying *he,*" Rob reminded her. "Did you see his face? Are you sure it was a man?"

"No." Eugenia accepted a toasted muffin. "Any jam for this? But it had to have been somebody strong enough to carry me; I'm not delicate, you know. And I don't remember seeing his face. Whoever it was must have worn something — maybe a mask or a scarf to cover his features.

"And there's something else —" Eugenia

paused in mid-bite. "That raincoat — it was slick, kind of shiny."

Rob looked at me and shrugged. "I keep one hanging by the back door, but Ethelene uses it half the time. Well, I guess we'll have to do a 'slicker check'! Go from closet to closet until we find the guilty party."

Rob poured Mrs. T.S.S. another cup of cider and pulled his chair closer to hers. "How long have you lived here at the tavern, Eugenia?"

"Almost seven years now, or will be in November. A few years before I had stayed here for the wedding when Charlotte — she was my niece, you know — married that fool Otto, and I fell in love with the place. Then later, when my husband passed on and I retired from my position at Huddleston's, I remembered Plumb-Nelly. I detest cooking, and it's much more personal here than a residential hotel — plus the rates are affordable."

"And you love it. And me. Admit it." Rob kissed her cheek.

Eugenia chewed on her muffin and nodded agreeably.

"I've heard of Huddleston's," I said. "That's a department store — in Raleigh, isn't it? What did you do there?"

"Well, my title was executive secretary,

but I really ran the place. To tell you the truth, I'm surprised they're still in business. Wouldn't shock me at all to hear they've gone under." And she smiled at the thought of it.

"Has anything like this ever happened to you before?" Rob asked. "Let's face it, Eugenia, somebody wants you out of the way. Do you have any idea why?"

"No, I can't imagine. Why, you know I'm the easiest person in the world to get along with!"

"I think it's because you know something," I said. "Remember, Eugenia, you said yourself Sheri was killed because she saw who drained the brake fluid from my car. Think. What did you say or do in the last day or so? Something nobody knew before."

"Dahlia Brown!" Rob stood so quickly, he almost knocked over his chair. "You recognized Dahlia Brown! Remember? You saw her in a play before she came to Fiddler's Glen . . . which means you might remember some of the other actors as well."

"Mason," I said. "It always comes back to Mason."

Of course I couldn't explain about our mysterious quest for Mason without going back to the beginning, or at least to the time when Mama Kate learned that her sister was dead. "We found the name Mason in one of her letters," I said, trying to remember the exact wording. "Something like *What am I going to do about Mason?* And she mentions this person more than once. Could've been an actor."

Eugenia blinked at me over her cup. "And you think he might still be around?"

"Or she," Rob said. "Mason might have been a stage name."

"We do have one clue," I said. "*The Bugle* gives an account of a party for Lucy given here a few weeks before Dahlia Brown was killed, and one of the guests was an actor named Hal Templeton. It might be worthwhile to talk with him if we just knew where to find him."

Eugenia set aside her cup. "Good grief, that was fifty years ago! Besides, somebody around here seems to get a little upset when you begin to get curious."

Rob smiled. "And that's where you come in," he said.

Since Eugenia had been attacked the night before, she shouldn't be in danger, Rob assured her. And besides, he and I would be there to protect her, he said. After all, didn't we save her last night?

I couldn't bring myself to tell Eugenia she had really been rescued by a ghost. "Don't worry about it, Eugenia," I said. "If you're nervous about it, we'll just have to find another way."

"Nonsense! I've never been nervous a day in my life! Angry, maybe, but never nervous. And now I'm just plain blood-boiling mad!" Eugenia gripped the arms of her chair. "Now, just what do you want me to say?"

Eugenia's well-wishers seemed to fill the house that night when she came downstairs on Bailey's arm to hold court in the front parlor. We had told them the truth about the drugged tea and the arson attempt in the old barn. That way, we hoped whoever did it would be on his (or her?) best behavior, and the innocent would be watchful as well.

"Have they learned anything from that raincoat they found?" Otto Millsap asked Rob with just enough of a smile to be annoying. "Heard it belonged to you."

"That's right. It was in the toolshed." Rob spoke evenly. He didn't smile, didn't even blink. "I keep it hanging in the back hall, so just about anybody could have taken it . . . or it might have been me."

Eugenia laughed and whacked him heartily on the arm, but Otto looked a little paler than usual.

"Do they know what was in that tea you drank?" Grace asked. "Lord, I hope it wasn't one of those drugs that drives you crazy — you know, makes you see visions and things like that."

"Nonsense! Sam Molloy says it's just an ordinary ingredient found in most sleeping pills. Almost anybody could get it. Doctors prescribe it a lot for people who aren't sleeping well." Eugenia blinked at her. "How've you been sleeping, Grace? I should think you have chronic insomnia since you caused Charlotte to crash into that tree."

"Cheese dip?" I stuck a plate in her face. "Try some, Eugenia. This is that recipe Ethelene cut out of *McCall's*."

Delaney stooped over me to scoop up dip with a cracker. "Eat, drink, and be merry, for tomorrow you may die!" she said, popping it into her mouth.

Bailey frowned. "Delaney, that's not funny!"

"I didn't mean it to be. But why should you worry? Obviously it's not men this person is after. I could be next."

Maybe so, I thought, but I happened to know Delaney had a prescription for sleeping tablets because I had seen her take them. And I had an idea the police knew about it too.

"I hear they found that photographer, the one who killed Sheri," Otto said.

"Then you didn't hear right," Chamblee Davenport told him. "Fellow had nothing to do with it. Somebody right here in Fiddler's Glen ran down Sheri." He looked around to give his statement time to sink in. "Probably somebody we all know."

"My goodness, Chamblee, you'll have us all looking over our shoulders," Lucy said, laughing. "Let's talk about something more cheerful, shall we?"

"Right." Rob jumped right in. "Tell us about that old musical you were talking about the other night, Eugenia. What else did they sing?"

"Oh, I don't know . . . a lot of hardy Mountie music, I think. It was most colorful. And the co-star — or at least I think it was the co-star — was very good-looking." She frowned as if she were straining to remember. "Hal . . . somebody. I wonder if he came here with the others."

"Hal?" Lucy looked at her husband. "Do you remember a Hal?"

"I do." Grace Millsap looked almost agreeable. "He was short, and kind of cute. Used

261

to pay me to iron his shirts. Good tipper too."

"Wonder whatever happened to him?" Eugenia said.

"Good Lord, who knows?" Kirby Whitworth helped himself to a glass of sherry. "I'd forgotten all about him."

"Well, I hadn't," Grace informed us. "He married a girl from North Wilkesboro — used to bring her here now and then. I think he still lives there — did dinner theater for a while."

Lucy laughed. "You mean he's still acting? Well, good for him! Kirby, we were up there for *Fiddler on the Roof* — when was it, two or three years ago? Wonder if he was in it."

"Is that theater still in business?" Rob asked.

"Was last summer," Delaney told him. "Play wasn't bad, but the food was awful."

I looked at Rob, who was trying to avoid Eugenia's eyes. At least we knew where to go from here.

I had started into the kitchen to help with dinner, when I felt a hand close over my arm. I knew whose hand it was. Eugenia shoved me into a chair. "We've almost an hour before time to eat," she said. "Ethelene can do without you for a while. Now, shut up and deal!"

Chapter Twenty-four

The manager of Footlights, a dinner theater near Wilkesboro, was a friend of Hal Templeton's, we learned. "But he's in failing health, I'm afraid," he told us over the phone. "Can't keep up the pace onstage, but he does what he can — helps with props when he's able — things like that."

And since the next day was a Saturday, Rob and I, with Eugenia dictating directions from the backseat, made the hour-long drive to find him.

I was afraid we would be disturbing an invalid when we located the rustic cottage where the former actor lived with his wife, and was surprised to find a small, fit-looking man edging the borders by the brick walkway. He brushed off his hands and came to greet us, leaving no doubt by his voice and carriage that he would be at home on the stage. "I'm glad you could come; don't get too many visitors out here anymore.

"How about a cup of coffee?" he asked, leading us inside. "I think Betty put on a pot just a while ago."

Betty Templeton, who seemed just as charming as her husband, served homemade cinnamon rolls and coffee, and after preliminary pleasantries let her husband do most of the talking.

"Of course I remember Dahlia Brown," he said, casting a discerning glance at me. "You look very much like her, you know. Was she a relative?"

I nodded. "My grandmother's sister. She never even knew how or when her sister died until recently, and I'm trying to find out how it happened. What things were like at the tavern . . . I hope you can help us."

He sighed and shook his head. "That was when? The mid-thirties, wasn't it? My Lord, we were young! I just had my eightieth birthday, you know; that should give you an idea how long ago that was."

He frowned. "Your aunt died in a fall, they said. To tell you the truth, I never did understand it. Some say she heard the fiddler — or thought she did, but Dahlia was too practical to wander alone at night."

"She was with a group of performers before she came to Plumb-Nelly," Rob said. "We thought you might have been with the same company."

To my surprise, Hal Templeton laughed.

"I was the greenest of greenhorns! Plumb-Nelly was my first experience outside of college and community theater. I remember how excited I was — and proud — to actually get paid for it!"

Eugenia dabbed at her mouth with a dainty napkin. She had already eaten two cakes and was eyeing a third. "Then you didn't know Virginia's aunt before she came to Fiddler's Glen?"

"No, but I remember what fun we had while we were there. Your aunt was young and pretty and she loved to have a good time. Had a tart tongue too, and didn't hesitate to use it." He laughed. "Told a heckler once that when the Lord was handing out mouths, he must have thought He said *sows* and asked for a big, fat, dirty one! That was the last we heard out of him!

"Plumb-Nelly was a special place — or it seemed so to me. The Davenports treated us more like house guests than hired help, and we had access to the tennis courts — there were horses too — and parties. Wonderful parties!" Hal Templeton shook his head. "It was a shame it had to end that way. You know, I always thought Dahlia and Chamblee Davenport would . . . well, there was definitely something there."

"Mr. Templeton, do you have any idea

where Dahlia Brown performed before she came to Plumb-Nelly? We're trying to locate a person who may have been a member of that cast. Someone named Mason."

"Mason? No, I don't remember a Mason, but I do remember your aunt telling me about some of the places she'd played. Small towns, resorts mostly; she saved all the programs — kept a scrapbook. She was almost as proud as I was. And she had talent too. Who knows . . ."

"I don't suppose you know what happened to that scrapbook," I said.

"Well, since they couldn't locate her family, I suppose Lucy kept it. They were friends, you know. She was really broken up when Dahlia died."

Hal Templeton stayed with Showtime South for a few more years until he married Betty and went into the insurance business with her father, he told us. But he remained active in community theater, and later, when he retired, resumed minor roles in productions at Footlights.

"It's been a good life," he said, walking us to the door. "We never had children, so the theater kind of took their place, I guess. I still enjoy it, even though I can't bustle about the way I used to." Hal Templeton glanced at his watch and smiled. "And now, in about two seconds Betty will tell me it's time for my pills."

I heard her calling his name as we reached the car.

"We have to find that scrapbook," I said as we drove back to the tavern. "Do you suppose it's still around?"

"It depends on how thoroughly the Davenports clean house," Rob said. "Bailey told me that after his mother remarried, they got rid of a lot of things. If it's anywhere, it would be in the attic."

"Lucy might know," Eugenia said. "Do you want me to ask her?"

"That's all right, thanks," I said. "I'm sure she must suspect I'm related to Dahlia Brown; I might as well come clean. After all, what else can happen?"

But the Whitworths had left that morning, Bailey told us, to attend a fund-raising barbecue for their son, Woodrow, and weren't expected back until Monday. And the whole county, it seemed, caught wind of Ethelene's spaghetti sauce and turned up for dinner that night. I wouldn't have had time to look for the scrapbook if somebody had drawn me a map.

The hangers-on after dinner were more in a mood for games than for musical entertainment — which suited me fine, so we divided into teams for Trivial Pursuit, crowding around the fireplace in the parlor. Bailey and I were on the same team, and every time I managed to answer correctly, he rewarded me with a hug, always with a significant look at Rob. I didn't mind the hugs as much as I disliked his annoying attitude. Yet I hated to make an issue of it in public. Bailey was deliberately trying to provoke Rob's anger.

And he nearly succeeded. Rob's usually calm face turned a mottled pink, and a muscle twitched in his jaw. "Hey, it's a game," I whispered to Rob, who was on the other team. Bailey had gone into the kitchen for soft drinks, and the two of us huddled over the sheet music at the piano as if we had forgotten to put it away. "Bailey just likes to win, that's all. Don't let him get to you."

"Well, he's not going to win this time," Rob said, forcing me to meet his eyes. I knew he wasn't talking about Trivial Pursuit.

When Eugenia excused herself for the night, I did the same, and made sort of an issue out of helping her from her chair. I thought she was going to hit me with her cane. "What did you do that for?" she bellowed when we got out into the hall. "I'm not a cripple, you know!"

"Will you hush? Can't you see what was

going on in there? If I didn't leave, I was afraid the two of them would really get into it."

Eugenia giggled. Well, almost giggled. "Do you really think so? Well, shoot! Let's go back. I don't want to miss this."

I blocked her way with my arm. "No you don't! You gave me the excuse I needed. Besides, we both could use the rest. There's no telling what might happen around here next."

But everything seemed peaceful, for a while at least, until the next afternoon. Rob had driven Eugenia to a wedding in a nearby town, and Delaney planned to spend the day "up to her elbows" in clay, she announced. I didn't want to be left alone in the house with Bailey, so I put in a few hours at *The Bugle* checking copy on the next week's ads. It was almost twilight when I started back, and even though I wasn't hungry, I stopped at a fast-food place for a salad so I wouldn't get home before the others.

But I didn't wait long enough. Dark shadows draped the lawn as I pulled into my customary parking place and looked about. Rob and Eugenia still had not returned, and Delaney's parking space was vacant. Nor did I see Bailey's white Honda Accord.

No lights shone in the kitchen, but I could see a lamp burning in the front hall. The place seemed unusually dark, and at that point I think I would have been glad to see even Bailey Davenport. I cut across the backyard, wading through brown leaves under the big oaks, and hurried up the walk. I had almost reached the steps when I heard it. The strains of a violin.

I dream of Jeanie with the light brown hair . . . The old refrain surrounded me with its poignancy; the heavy sadness seemed to drip from the trees, to move in sticky measures among the shadows at my feet. Where was it coming from? This time I had heard no hoofbeats, only the notes from a phantom fiddle.

I inched backward and nearly fell over the step. I could visualize him there: the spirit of Willie Hugh Jordan in his tattered Confederate gray. As the music grew louder, I began to hope it was a ghost. I would be in more danger from a human than an apparition, but would I be safer inside the tavern or out?

If only I could get inside, bolt the heavy doors, manage somehow to get to the security of my room . . . I scrambled up the steps and grabbed the doorknob with a sweaty hand. It was locked.

Come on, Virginia, you have a key. In that little compartment in your purse. Quit shaking! Open your purse; take your time now. You know it's there. Ah . . . now, slowly insert it in the lock. Nothing's going to hurt you. Soon you'll be safe . . . soon . . . soon . . .

I sighed out loud when the door swung open, then darted inside, bolting it behind me. The house sounded hollow as I ran through the empty hallway and up the stairs. I called out to Bailey — to anybody, but no one answered. I wondered if Dahlia was there. Probably not. I didn't sense her presence.

Why hadn't somebody thought to leave a light on in the upstairs hall? It was as dark as a vampire's closet up there. I held to the smooth mahogany railing, felt the massive square newel post at the top. Soon I would be in my room, and I was never coming out again! I would have my meals served there, grow old huddled under the blue patchwork quilt.

I was halfway down the corridor when the front door opened. I heard the heavy wood slam against the wall, footsteps on the stairs below. And I screamed.

Chapter Twenty-five

"Ginger! My God, you nearly scared me to death!" Bailey overtook me at the end of the hall and clasped me by the shoulders. "What's wrong? Why are you screaming?" He switched on a lamp and looked at me. "Are you all right? Where's Rob? Where's Eugenia?"

"I don't know." I shook my head and sat in the little Victorian chair that stood in the corner. The shade from the hurricane lamp glowed with a rosy warmth that seemed to relax me. I waited until my breathing slowed. "I'm okay," I said finally. "I thought you were the fiddler — or somebody worse."

He started to smile. "The fiddler? You're not serious?"

"Didn't you hear it? The music. Out back — everywhere!"

"I just got here; been at the library all afternoon. You must have parked out back. I didn't see your car, and when I unlocked the front door I heard someone upstairs. . . ."

I nodded. "Me. When you came up those stairs I thought my number was up. Bailey, why is somebody doing this to me?"

He pulled me to my feet and would have taken me in his arms, but I moved away. "Let's go downstairs. I could use a cup of tea," I said. "Not sassafras!"

"This fiddler — was he playing the same thing?" Bailey stood at the kitchen window while we waited for the kettle to boil.

" 'Jeanie with the Light Brown Hair.' But I couldn't tell where it was coming from."

"Did you see anyone?"

"No, there wasn't a horseman this time, just the music. That was enough!"

He stood beside me as I poured steaming water into the pot. "It's about that girl in the painting, isn't it? Dahlia Brown. Why is she so important to you?"

He seemed harmless, even comforting, standing there. Bailey Davenport. I had known him longer than I'd known most of my friends. "She was my aunt," I said. "Well, my great-aunt, really."

"And is that why you're here?"

"Partly. I didn't mean to stay." I smiled at him. "Your offer was just too good to refuse."

"And what about my other offer?" I could feel him standing behind me. Close. His hands were on my waist. His lips on my neck.

I turned and took his face in my hands.

"Bailey, I can't. I'm sorry. I just don't feel that way about you."

"And Rob?" He stiffened under my touch.

"I don't think Rob feels that way about you either." I kissed him lightly on the lips and backed away, watching his face, waiting for him to laugh. He didn't disappoint me.

"I guess I set myself up for that," Bailey said, pouring the dark tea into mugs. "It is Rob Quillian, isn't it?"

God forbid, I didn't even have to think about it. "Yes." I took a swallow of tea and smiled. "But he doesn't know it yet."

"Who doesn't know what?" Eugenia banged into the room through the kitchen door, followed by Rob, who looked as if he'd been confined with a crying baby and a barking dog. "Why is this place so dark? Where is everybody?"

"It's Sunday," I reminded her. "What happened to you?"

Rob poured a glass of milk and drank thirstily. "You wouldn't believe it! My tire went flat on me, and somebody's taken my jack. Had to walk two miles to find a store that carried that sealer that comes in a can."

"Where did this happen?" Bailey asked. And for the first time in weeks, the antagonism was gone from his voice. I wondered if Rob noticed it too.

"Just a few blocks from the church. I picked up some things from a nursery there while Eugenia was at the wedding, and met her in the church parking lot afterward. Funny. A big nail in my back tire — must've been in there for a while. Can't imagine where I picked it up."

"I can," I said. "Somebody put it where you wouldn't miss it."

Eugenia opened the refrigerator. "Somebody did what?"

I told them about coming home to the dark, empty house and hearing the music. "Somebody wanted to be sure I'd be alone."

Rob turned to Bailey. "Do you know anybody who plays the violin?"

"In this family? You know we're all tone deaf! You and Ginger are the only musicians around."

"But there's a fiddle in your study, isn't there?" Eugenia finished off a cold drumstick and went to the sink for water. "Blast it! This thing's still leaking! Thought you said you fixed it . . . I've seen a fiddle, haven't I?" she asked Bailey. "Hanging on that wall right over your bookshelves."

"Oh, that!" Bailey seemed as surprised as I was. "That belonged to my great-grandpa Josh Davenport. He used to play for square dances." He laughed. "Aunt Lucy says he made them all take lessons, but they gave up on her before she got very far."

"You mean they all played?" I tried not to sound accusing.

"Not really. My granddaddy could squeak out 'Skip to My Lou,' but I don't think Uncle Chamblee or Aunt Lucy got even that far." Bailey shrugged. "Look, I don't like this any better than you do, believe me. I really didn't think about that fiddle. When something's around all the time, you more or less forget about it."

Eugenia looked up. "Maybe it's not around."

But it was. We found it hanging in its usual place to the right of the door — just within reach, and there wasn't a speck of dust on it.

"Well, what do you think?" Rob asked as we sat on the front steps eating apples. The light from the parlor kept it from being completely dark, and a quarter moon seemed to hang from the tip of the red bud tree.

"About Bailey? I don't think we have to worry about him. Besides, anybody could have taken that fiddle if they wanted to, but I don't think they did."

Rob tossed his apple core into the bushes. "Don't tell me you think it was another ghost?"

"No, I think it's a tape. And you don't have to be a musician to play it."

He pulled me closer. "Well, that lets me out!" He kissed my ear. "What's with you and Bailey?"

"What do you mean?"

"I don't know . . . he just seemed more relaxed some how. More like his old self."

I put my head on his shoulder. "I told him I didn't love him."

"Really?"

"Really. I told him there was someone else."

"You'd better not mess with me, Ginger Cameron," Rob said.

"Oh? I thought that was sort of what you had in mind."

"I'm waiting," Rob said later. He draped his jacket around me, but I didn't need it. Gradually the ocean's roaring subsided inside my head. If this kept up, I would have to invest in diving gear. I laced my fingers in his. "Waiting for what?"

"For you to ask me what I'm doing here. Why I'm wasting my life doing yard work. Don't tell me you aren't curious."

"I was going to get to that," I said. "But not tonight." I didn't want to spoil the moment by being practical.

"I'd like to tell you anyway." Rob led the way into the empty parlor. It was not yet ten o'clock, but everyone had gone to bed, except for Delaney, but I had seen her handsome, bearded potter, and I had a pretty good idea she'd done the same. Only not at Plumb-Nelly.

I sat in Eugenia's chair by the window. "I'm all ears."

Rob gave me an appraising look. "Oh, no, you're not." He turned away and moved to the fireplace, where he put both hands on the mantel and addressed the cold grate. "I was in with a Charlotte law firm for almost five years: good practice, good money. There was even a girl — well, a woman. Jessica. We were engaged."

The pain of Jessica soaked into my bones like acid, and I bent my head so he couldn't see my face. I didn't want to know, but I had to ask. "What happened?"

"I burned out, I guess. It was too heavy — all that paperwork and no personal contact. It wasn't for me. It became drudgery. I had to get away."

Rob moved to the piano, but he didn't sit down, just stood with one hand touching the silent keyboard. "I stuck it out for a year after my grandmother died; then when Barney died a few months later, I buried him there in the backyard and sold the house.

"Jessica didn't understand, and I don't blame her. Why should I give up a profitable law practice where I was almost certain to become a partner? And give it up for what? To wander? Commune with nature?" Rob looked up and laughed. "Jessica wasn't one for communing with nature! And frankly, I didn't know what I wanted to do. I just knew I had to get away — for a while at least." He threw up his hands. "And here I am!"

I went over and put my arms around him. "And so am I. What are we going to do about it?"

He didn't answer for a very long time.

"Do you think Bailey and his sister would ever consider selling Plumb-Nelly?" Rob asked later as we cuddled on the sofa listening to the old house grow quiet around us.

"Why? Are you thinking of becoming an innkeeper?"

"Why not? It suits me, and this place — well, it has an abiding beauty, a serenity —"

"Serenity? Oh, sure! Ask me about it. Ask Eugenia. I've felt more serene in a traffic jam with a tablespoon of gas in the tank."

"But that has nothing to do with the place: the house, the land around it." Rob examined my fingers, tucked my hand in his. "There's something else here too, Ginger. And whatever it is, it's what I need."

I knew what he meant. When I first came back to Plumb-Nelly, I had felt it too: the gold-green tranquility of the place had washed over me as I stood on the hillside. "I think Delaney would sell in a minute," I said. "But I don't know about Bailey. What about all those sleeping Davenports on the hill back there? Do you think he could leave them behind? They're too much a part of him, Rob."

He just smiled. "We'll see. I'm not greedy; I'm not interested in all the land — just the part the tavern's on, and maybe a few acres around it. I made some investments that did fairly well, and then there's the money from the sale of Gram's house. I'd like to make them an offer, but it depends on you. How would you feel about staying?"

I couldn't think of being anyplace without him, but I had never considered my position at *The Bugle* as being permanent. Chamblee Davenport was ready to retire completely, devote more time to painting. And I liked the Cuthberts, who owned the paper, and the young reporter who wrote most of the copy. It had the potential to become a strong voice in the area — if someone took the time to boost advertising and circulation. I had a feeling that someone might be me. "What about your practice?" I asked. "Will you give it up completely?"

"Certainly not! After all that work? I could set up a practice here. There's a need for it, and it's a central location." He cupped my face in his hands. "What do you say, Virginia Cameron?"

"I say we talk to Bailey tomorrow," I said. Now that Rob was rid of his ghosts, maybe I could banish mine. And the key to it, I hoped, was in a scrapbook in the attic.

Chapter Twenty-six

I couldn't go to sleep. *If that scrapbook is here, it's in the attic,* Eugenia had said. But where? It was a big attic. And dark. Besides, the house was old. They had been accumulating things at Plumb-Nelly for over two hundred years.

I watched the dark square of window grow gray with morning. In another hour I should be able to see.

The racket under my window woke me, and I looked out to see Ethelene banging her shoes together, then shaking her umbrella before she came inside to start breakfast. I looked at my clock: six-thirty on the dot. If I hurried, I should be able to spend an hour or so in the attic — if I just knew where to start.

Delaney's door was closed, but her car was parked in its usual place. I had no idea when she had come in, but I knew better than to wake her. I found Bailey in the kitchen, downing a glass of orange juice before his early class, and wondered how he would greet me, but he seemed marginally cheerful for such an early hour and even asked how I slept. "No more serenades, I hope? No phantom riders in the night?"

"I can see you haven't lost any sleep over this," I said. "Surely you don't think I'm making it up."

Bailey reached out to touch me, then changed his mind. "As a matter of fact, it worries the hell out of me. I didn't mean to be flippant, Ginger. I just hate to see you living in fear." He rinsed his glass in the sink. "The police are coming by this morning. Said they'd be here before you left for work. They want to check the area, see if they can find where the music came from."

I shrugged. "They won't find anything. Whoever's doing this isn't going to leave evidence around."

"But what possible purpose would anyone have —"

"They expected me to follow it — follow the sound, like my aunt was supposed to have done. And if anything happens to me, they can blame it on my wild hallucinations. Well, she *did* hear the fiddler, you know!" I shrugged. "Or maybe it was meant to scare me to death." And it nearly succeeded. I thought of the dark, deserted tavern and of the person waiting there, knowing I would be alone.

"Bailey, do you know of anybody in your family named Mason?" I said, hoping he wouldn't ask why I wanted to know.

But he shook his head. "No, the only person I know with that family connection would be Eugenia."

I think I gasped. "Eugenia?"

He nodded. "Her grandmother was a Mason. Haven't you ever noticed the initials on that huge locket she wears? I asked her about it once. They stand for Anne Mason Tyler — her father's mother."

I had to sit down. No! Not Eugenia. Had the woman staged her own abduction in the barn? But she would have to have had an accomplice to stack straw outside the door — unless she knew another way out of the storage room. Eugenia had admitted meeting Dahlia when she was a young girl. Was there more to their relationship? Something she wasn't telling us?

Rob came through the swinging door; his arm brushed my shoulder. "Good thing I brought those chair cushions inside yesterday. I think porch-sitting weather's over for a while." His tone was light, almost impersonal. I wondered if he had mentioned his plans to Bailey.

Rob held the door for Ethelene, who had been to the pantry for jam. "Good morning, beautiful!" he said, kissing her on the cheek and looking at me the whole time.

"Get outta my way," Ethelene said. "If you really want to get on my good side, go fix that sink. It's leaking all over the place. And why are all of you hanging around here? Breakfast won't be ready for another twenty minutes."

She looked as if she might ask me to help, so I started making my exit. "Do you have any idea where they might have stored my aunt's things?" I asked Bailey. I had to find that scrapbook. Today.

"Your aunt? Oh, you mean Dahlia Brown. Good Lord, Ginger, that was a million years ago!"

"I know, but I thought you might've run across something when you cleaned out your attic . . . do you think Delaney —"

"Delaney probably hasn't been in that attic since she used to play dress-up." Bailey paused, obviously seeing the disappointment on my face. "Why not ask Uncle Chamblee? It's pretty obvious he was in love with your aunt."

I nodded silently. I wouldn't see Chamblee Davenport for a couple of hours. I looked to Rob for help.

"I'll give you a hand up there for a little while if Bailey doesn't mind," he offered.

"We don't want to disturb family keepsakes."

"Tell you what . . ." Bailey stood with his hands in his pockets. "Why don't you start in that left front section? The room below it's empty right now, so you won't bother anybody. I stacked I don't know how many boxes over there, some of them filled with stuff going back to Noah." He lifted down cups from the cabinet and set them on a tray. "And I'll give Aunt Lucy a call. If there is anything up there, she could tell us what to look for."

The dim lighting did little to illuminate the gloom of the attic, and dreary rain streamed down windows dingy with cobwebs. No sunlight here. The boxes Bailey had told us about might not have gone back to Noah, but I found a set of encyclopedias that spelled airplane *aeroplane* and a stack of letters written before the War Between the States.

I had told Rob what Bailey said about Eugenia's locket, but he didn't seem at all concerned. "She probably didn't think it was worth mentioning," he explained with a shrug. "If Eugenia thought there was a connection, she'd have told you."

But not if she had something to hide, I thought.

"Think of all the stories this place could

tell," I said instead. "I wish I had the time to really get into some of this stuff."

But Rob didn't answer. He was absorbed in somebody's college annual dated 1923. "Look at this car," he said when I interrupted him. "Can you imagine what that would be worth today?"

"That is not why we're here though — remember?"

He pulled me to him and kissed me, and I had to remind myself that this was a working day. My hands were numb from cold and the attic was musty and feathered with dust, but I was happy being near him, hearing the rain beat down on the roof just above us.

Rob slipped his hand underneath my sweater at the small of my back. "You only wanted me up here so you could have your way with me," he whispered.

"You're right." I gave him a quick kiss and a sound shove. "Your way is over there, and my way is over here. I have to get to work on time and you promised Ethelene you'd fix that dripping sink."

I dragged out a promising-looking box and dug into it while Rob reluctantly investigated a pile of shapes in the corner. Thirty minutes later I had unearthed Chamblee Davenport's high school valedictory speech and the minutes of the local chapter of the United Daughters of the Confederacy from 1926 to 1929. Rob discovered an ancient croquet set, a boy scout manual that had been Bailey's father's, and a tennis racquet that must have belonged to Adam himself.

We had decided it was time to call it quits for a while when Bailey called from below to tell us the police were here.

I left two policemen tiptoeing through the muck in the backyard and drove the few miles to *The Bugle* while picking attic grime from my dark green slacks. Chamblee Davenport had a touch of bronchitis, I was told, and wouldn't be in that day. I didn't bother to try to hide my disappointment. The police didn't seem to doubt my story about the eerie fiddle music, but I really didn't think they would turn up any clues. The candlestick that had been left with Eugenia in the barn was wiped clean of prints — except for mine. And whoever paid me a visit the night before had been careful not to step in moist places. We were going to have to expose our intimidating phantom some other way.

I was almost certain the secret of Dahlia Brown's death was in an old theater program, and I hung on to the belief that either Chamblee or his sister Lucy had cared enough about her to save it. If I couldn't get in touch with Lucy by noon, I decided, I would call her brother at home — bronchitis, or no bronchitis.

But there was a message on my desk when I returned from my morning calls at a little after ten. Lucy Whitworth wanted me to phone her at home.

She sounded excited when she realized who was calling, and her voice took on a girlish quality. "Bailey tells me he might be selling the old place to Rob Quillian," she confided. "Has he mentioned it to you?"

"Rob did say he was interested," I admitted. "Do you really think he'll sell?"

"Well, Delaney certainly doesn't want it, and frankly, I think Bailey resents being tied down." She paused, and I thought I heard a nervous little laugh. "But that's not why I called. It's about your aunt. Bailey told me your great-aunt was Dahlia Brown. . . . I should have known right away who you were, Virginia. I'll have to admit, it did occur to me."

"I hope you saved some of her things," I said. "I was told there was a scrapbook."

"I believe there was . . . and some photographs and a few other keepsakes. You should have those. I just packed her things away in a suitcase, hoping that someday we'd know where to send them." Lucy paused. "I understand her sister — your grandmother — is still living. I'd like very much to meet her."

Yes, yes, I assured her. Mama Kate would like to meet her too. Now, about that scrapbook. . . .

"The last time I saw that old suitcase it was in that stack of things in the attic, somewhere on the right, over the kitchen."

"Can you give me an idea what to look for?" My fingers played "Pink Cadillac" on the counter.

"My goodness, seems everything was drab back then. Just an old worn-out brown bag. I know I saw it when I was helping Bailey get rid of some things up there four or five years ago. Somewhere against that back wall . . . it's difficult to say exactly —

"Why don't I do this? I have a meeting in half an hour, but I should be through by twelve-thirty. Why don't I just meet you there at about one? We can look for it together?"

"One? That would be fine," I said, thanking her. I looked at my watch. It was fifteen to eleven. That would mean I'd have to wait two hours and fifteen minutes.

I stuck my head in the editor's door. "I'm going out on calls," I lied. "See you after lunch."

★ ★ ★

The sun was shining as I started up the drive to Plumb-Nelly, and I glanced at the upper porch just to see if my aunt was waiting there, but there was no one about. Not even a ghost.

The police had left. Ron Slater had promised to call me if they found anything suspicious, and since I hadn't heard from him, that must have meant they didn't. I wasn't surprised. I found Anita alone in the kitchen, looking hopefully into a pot of something that smelled like onion soup. They were supposed to serve chicken salad in those cute little pastry shells, she said, but Ethelene had dropped the last jar of mayonnaise and gone to The Store for more, leaving her in charge.

"You seem to be doing fine," I said. There usually weren't too many for lunch on Mondays, and I knew there was a frozen fruit salad ready to serve.

"Yeah, but there's no water . . ."Anita nodded toward the sink, and for the first time I saw Rob's wrench lying on the floor along with a section of pipe. "He had to go all the way into Morganton to get a part. What if he doesn't get back before noon?"

"He will. Look, there's something I absolutely *have* to do," I told her. "But if disaster strikes, I'll be in the attic."

She nodded. She didn't seem relieved.

I stuck my head back around the swinging door. "By disaster, I mean hurricane, fire, or flood!" I added. "Nothing less."

I remembered how dark it had been that morning and grabbed Rob's big flashlight from the back hall before going upstairs. I thought about asking Eugenia why she didn't tell me about her grandmother's name, but her closed door reminded me she had been invited to a bridge luncheon in town that day. I was alone in the old house, except for a nervous maid two floors below. And the ghost of Dahlia Brown.

I think I expected her to be there, sitting on top of that old suitcase like a mermaid on a rock, but she wasn't. The dangling overhead bulb cast a splash of yellow light in the center of the room, but the corners remained dark. I switched on my flashlight, feeling a little resentful at my aunt's neglect of late. After all, this was her problem. Wasn't it? And I could almost hear my grandmother's voice. *Not anymore, Virginia.*

I tied my one and only designer silk scarf around my hair and began to sort through the stack. I found a heavy green piece of luggage with somebody's old prom dresses inside, and a couple of hat boxes with hats that must have been from the forties, but the brown bag wasn't there. I squinted at my watch. I had been there nearly an hour, and had looked in everything at least twice. Could Lucy Whitworth have been wrong? Or perhaps someone had moved it.

And then I knew she was there. I didn't see her at first; it was a gradual awareness. A peaceful feeling came over me — a little like the cathedral calmness that comes from walking in the woods, and I saw a daisy at my feet. And then another. The scattered trail led to a dusty mound to the left of the door behind what had once been the kitchen chimney. The pantry, and then the back porch would be just below me.

I tugged at a rolled-up carpet and hoisted it aside with strength I seldom used. Underneath was a battered trunk that looked as if it might have been around at the beginning of the century. The nineteenth century. And inside the trunk I found the suitcase. It was brown with a light tan stripe, and the imitation leather had peeled from the edges. I pulled it into the light, and as I did, I saw her standing there. Only for a second, but I knew she was urging me to hurry.

The suitcase wasn't locked, and the scrapbook lay at the bottom underneath a bundle of fusty clothing. I carried it into the light, where a sepia snapshot of my grandmother as a little girl fell into my hands. There was another of the two sisters together, made when they were small — before their parents died, and then a third of a group of young people sitting on the steps of a house. In a larger photograph still enclosed in a brown folder I recognized a young Lucy Davenport on the running board of what would now be considered an antique car, while a much slimmer Kirby peered under the hood. WHITWORTH FORD and a street address was painted on the side in dark lettering. Was this the first of Kirby's successful ventures? I laid the pictures gently aside.

The theater programs had once been pasted to the pages, but time and the dryness of the attic had loosened them and they shifted when I opened the book, some of them slipping to the floor. The cheap black paper between the covers had disintegrated so badly that it fell apart in my lap, scattering little powdery pieces on the attic floor. The programs — there were eight of them — were brown-mottled, but the print was still legible. The actor whose first name was Mason appeared in the first three productions when my great-aunt joined the company in Raleigh, and then again in the musical Eugenia had seen in Asheville. He wasn't mentioned after that.

I made a packet of the photographs and

programs and tucked it into the pocket of my blazer, then hurriedly tossed what was left of the scrapbook back into the brown bag, leaving a nest of crumbled black paper beneath the light. My hands were numb with cold and I began to shiver, more from fear than from the frigid attic temperature. I felt drained of strength, as if I had been sick for a long time, and I knew I had to get out of that attic. Now.

The name on the program was Mason *Woodrow.*

I sensed Dahlia Brown beside me, almost touching me, or as close as she could come to that. I smelled her flowers, not fresh flowers, but blooms that had dried and fallen to bits. And then I heard footsteps on the stairs.

At first I thought it was Lucy, but she wasn't due for another half hour, and besides, the tread was too heavy. I switched off the light and hid in the dark nook behind the chimney, hoping whoever it was couldn't hear me breathing. My chest pumped like a bellows and there didn't seem to be any way to muffle the noise — short of not breathing at all. And if the person on the stairs was my aunt's killer, that choice might not be optional.

I closed my eyes, plastering myself against

the grimy brick as the attic door opened. If it were Rob, he would have called out long before. It wasn't Rob.

Chapter Twenty-seven

The overhead bulb still swayed on its long cord when he opened the door. I could see it moving back and forth, casting a slim shadow on the attic floor. He would know I was there. He would see the scraps of black paper, the open trunk. And me.

I heard him take a few hesitant steps. I couldn't see him, but I knew who it was. Who it had to be.

"Is anyone there? Virginia, is that you?" Kirby Whitworth moved to the center of the room, where I had examined the scrapbook, and I heard him switch on the light. And oh, dear Lord, he would see the trail of daisies! But when I looked down they were gone. If I peered around the chimney I would see him. I closed my eyes. Rob should be back by now, and Ethelene. It was twelve-thirty; guests would be arriving for lunch. The floors and walls of the tavern were thick and sturdy; still, I should have been able to hear some movement below. Where was everybody?

"Lucy told me you'd be here, but I didn't

expect you until later. This does make things rather difficult. . . ." He spoke as if he were discussing the weather. "Come now, Virginia!" There was laughter in his voice. "I know where you are. Please step out so we can talk."

The man sounded almost reasonable. And he must be at least seventy-five, maybe older. What harm could he do? But Kirby Whitworth was a gardener; he practically lived outdoors, and as far as I knew was in excellent physical shape. Also, he was half again as big as I was and a lot taller. I looked about for some kind of weapon. The heavy flashlight was on the other side of the room, the croquet mallet in the opposite corner. I would just have to slip past him — make a dash for the door.

"Ah, so there you are." He stood in front of me, blocking my way, and for a few seconds he reminded me of my grandfather with his nubby tan sweater and corduroy pants. But his smile . . . I didn't like his smile. And I certainly didn't like the way he stood between me and the door. I stepped to one side. "Please let me by."

He made no move to comply. "Of course. But first, if you don't mind, I'd like to have the things you took from the scrapbook."

"What scrapbook?"

He smiled. "Don't be coy. The little girl downstairs tells me you've been here well over an hour." He held out a hand. "If you please, Virginia. I really must have it."

"Well, I don't please!" I gave him a shove, but he didn't yield. "You killed her, didn't you? You killed my aunt out there in the barn. Why? What had she ever done to you?"

He seized my wrist and swung me around, pinning my hands behind me. I felt myself being propelled to the other side of the room — toward the windows and light. I screamed. Surely someone would hear me: Anita or Ethelene, a guest coming for lunch. At the edge of the driveway I saw Otto Millsap get into his car and drive away.

"I'm afraid you're wasting your breath," Kirby said. "There's no one downstairs to hear you. There's no water, you see. The hired girl was leaving when I got here, said Rob Quillian called and said he had to go all the way to Hickory to get that sink part."

"But Ethelene . . . there are people to feed . . ." I tried to pull away and felt a pain shoot through my wrist.

"Hard to serve meals if there's no water. Ethelene left a sign on the door. The girl — what's her name — Anita? Says Ethelene took a couple of hours off to see her podiatrist." The awful man chuckled. "You know how her feet give her trouble."

I slammed down on his instep with the heel of my shoe. He yelled and let go of my wrists for a second, but it wasn't long enough. I felt his arm circle my neck, and to my horror, he snatched the scarf from my head and slid it over my face and around my throat, tightening it when I tried to get away. I gasped for breath and fell to my knees, feeling like a dog on a choke chain.

"What are you going to do?" I was afraid to move, even to talk, but I didn't have a choice. "People are going to know you were here. The police were here this morning; they're coming back."

I saw him looking at the window and could guess what he was thinking. If he hurled me through the window, everyone would think I had jumped. Just like they had assumed my great-aunt had fallen from Devil's Bluff.

"Your fiddler story won't work this time," I told him. "I'm not the only person who knows how Dahlia Brown died."

I couldn't tell if he believed me or not. "Is that right?" he said.

He loosened his grip, and I sat up and rubbed my neck. "You missed a bead." I told him about the coral necklace. "You pushed her from the loft, didn't you?"

"You found a bead? One bead? But how did you know?" His voice kind of sputtered. Good. That had really shaken him!

"I doubt if you'd believe me," I said. "But why? Tell me why."

"Because she knew who he was." Lucy Whitworth stood in the attic doorway. I hadn't even heard her approaching. She walked toward us slowly, a sturdy, graceful woman with a sad face. "She knew he was already married to somebody else." She stood with her hand on his arm. Her head came to his shoulder. "Let her go, Kirby," she said, and he did.

"Dear God, Lucy! I didn't mean for you to know." Kirby Whitworth seemed to lose at least three inches in height, and for the first time he looked his age.

"But I have known — oh, not that you had anything to do with Dahlia's death, but that you had a family when we married, that you never bothered to get a divorce. I found out a few years ago when I helped Bailey straighten the attic when his mother married again. I'm sorry, Ginger, I tried to get here before he did — before you found it." Lucy moved between us, as if she could protect me from her husband's remorseless actions, but I didn't think it was necessary. Not now.

"I had never really looked through Dahlia's things. I just couldn't bring myself to do it after she died, and then — well, I guess I forgot them until I came across the scrapbook that day."

"You knew just from the theater programs?" I looked around for a box and sat on it. "How did you know who Mason Woodrow was?"

"Well, I didn't, of course — although Woodrow isn't a common name. It was that old snapshot — the one of the group of actors."

"Actors?"

"Sitting on the steps. They were holding a sign, didn't you notice? It was the cast of some theatrical; Kirby was right there in the middle — just behind Dahlia Brown. And he was always fond of quoting Shakespeare!" She looked at her husband. "I knew there must have been a reason he didn't tell me he knew her — or even that he'd acted, so I went back through the old programs; they gave a little background on all the major cast members, you see, and I found out Mason Woodrow was from a little town in Tennessee. It had to have been you, Kirby . . . and you told me you were from Chattanooga. . . . It took time, but I did some checking."

Lucy Whitworth paused, and when she began to speak again her voice sounded stronger. "You weren't from Chattanooga. The program listed your home as Luten's Mill, and you left a wife and two children behind in that town, Kirby. It may interest you to know that your wife had you declared dead after the required lapse of time and married a local doctor. And your girls, I hear, did very well without you. One became a teacher and the other a musician. They don't even know you exist."

"But why didn't you ever . . . I never realized —" Kirby sank his face into his hands.

"Because of our son. I kept it quiet because of Woodrow," Lucy said. "I wanted to give him the chance to go into politics if that's really what he wanted." Her voice grew softer. "And you were so young then! This happened such a long time ago; we'd been together fifty years. After all, how much longer do we have in this world?" She looked up at him, and I could see the tears in her eyes. "But murder? I can't live with murder, Kirby. Tell me the truth, *did* you kill Dahlia Brown?"

His silence was like a shout of admission. "She was going to tell you who I was — about my wife and children. She would have ruined everything . . . and I wanted you, Lucy. I loved you so much!"

Tiring of the theater and of being tied down to a family, Mason Woodrow had assumed a new identity and was selling cars in the area when he met young Lucy Davenport, never dreaming he would run across someone from his life as an actor. By the time Showtime South came to Plumb-Nelly, he had borrowed money to invest in a Ford dealership and was already seeing Lucy. Unfortunately, Dahlia Brown remembered he had a wife and children back in Tennessee.

And so on the pretext of asking her help in explaining the truth to Lucy, he managed to coax my aunt into the loft. Everyone else had left after the party that night, so there was no one to hear her scream, to see her pitch to the floor and die of a broken neck. Only her necklace broke as she fought against him, and the coral beads cascaded to the floor. Later that night Kirby had saddled a horse and taken my aunt's body to the place where they would find it. He must have destroyed all her identification as well.

"And the fiddler?" In the days before tape players, how had he managed that?

"Oh, Kirby could play the violin — piano

too," Lucy said. "When we were first married he used to belong to a trio, but he gave it up after a while." She glanced at her husband almost as if he were an afterthought. "And he knew how to handle a horse; Kirby could outride any of us — still can.

"If you'll look again at those programs," she said, "you'll see that in some of the variety shows the actors doubled as musicians. Kirby . . . excuse me, *Mason Woodrow* is listed as a violinist a couple of times."

"That was why you tried to get rid of Eugenia! You thought she might remember who you were." I waited for him to deny it, but he didn't.

"And Sheri," I said. "She saw you drain the brake fluid from my car. . . ."

Lucy lifted her head. "But I thought that was the man who followed you here. Oh, please, Kirby, you didn't have anything to do with Sheri's death?"

"She started asking questions . . . I knew it was just a matter of time before she said something. I told her it wasn't me, but she wouldn't believe me." Kirby shook his head. "You can't reason with a girl like that."

Lucy began to cry softly, and I stood and held her in my arms. "I can't take this!" she said. "I just can't take it."

Her husband, gray-faced, had shrunk to

his knees in the corner of the attic surrounded by two hundred years of the past. And it was the past that had brought him there. The glaring light bulb seemed to mock us amid all the shadows, and I reached up and turned it off. It was time to go. I put an arm around Lucy's waist and led her toward the door, but she stopped when we passed the trunk with Dahlia's suitcase crammed hastily inside. "What must she think of me?" she said. "Dahlia could be kind of blunt sometimes, but you always knew where you stood with her — and she was the most unselfish person I ever knew. Did you know that she once tried to give me those coral beads? It was the only nice thing she had." She shook her head at me. "I'll have to admit, I got right upset with your aunt about that! 'There are some things you just don't do,' I told her."

I almost smiled. And eavesdropping, Grace had heard every word.

"I didn't know . . . I just didn't know." Lucy looked about her as if she wasn't quite sure where she was. She seemed to have forgotten about her husband, who had managed to squirm behind an old bedstead and peered out at us from the spokes. It suited him somehow. "I would have done anything — I would have stopped him . . . I hope she knows that. Do you think she does?"

"She knows," I said. "It's all right now." And I knew that it was. Lucy knew it too. Could she see her there, just for an instant, with those glorious daisies in her arms?

"Why, Virginia, she smiled at you," Lucy said as we started again for the door.

"She smiled at us," I said. And I knew I wouldn't see Dahlia Brown again.

From the hall below I heard my sweetheart shouting, "Ginger, are you up there? I had to go all the way to Timbuktu to get that blasted pipe. You wouldn't believe the day I've had!"